Happy Days
and
Other Very Short Stories

Jake Allsop

PENGUIN BOOKS

PENGUIN BOOKS

Published by the Penguin Group
Penguin Books Ltd, 27 Wrights Lane, London w8 5TZ, England
Penguin Putnam Inc., 375 Hudson Street, New York, New York 10014, USA
Penguin Books Australia Ltd, Ringwood, Victoria, Australia
Penguin Books Canada Ltd, 10 Alcorn Avenue, Toronto, Ontario, Canada M4V 3B2
Penguin Books (NZ) Ltd, 182–190 Wairau Road, Auckland 10, New Zealand

Penguin Books Ltd, Registered Offices: Harmondsworth, Middlesex, England

First published in Penguin Books 1998
3 5 7 9 10 8 6 4 2

Text copyright © Jake Allsop, 1998

Set in 10/12pt Monotype Plantin
by Rowland Phototypesetting Ltd, Bury St Edmunds, Suffolk
Printed in England by Clays Ltd, St Ives plc

Contents

Happy Days
and Other
Very Short Stories

Introduction

The original idea for a book of short stories came to me when I was trying to keep up my slender knowledge of Portuguese and found that I could not easily sustain the reading of a story of normal length: I kept on forgetting the plot and the characters and, of course, the new words I encountered. If I had such problems, I reasoned, then so would students who were learning English. Since the first book of Very Short Stories, the idea has become a series. The present collection consists of twenty 600-word stories. They have various themes and settings, in the hope that students will be stimulated by this variety. Some stories are based on true incidents (for example, there really was a crazy taxi driver in Lubito called Cardosa; Grandma Pye's picture did move inexplicably the day before she died). The story 'It Will Do You Good' was inspired by an incident in Mark Twain's *Tom Sawyer*; the story 'Seeing Is Believing' by Robert Browning's poem *Tray*.

Wherever possible, the vocabulary and sentence constructions are within the range of a student with a limited command of English. Where lexical items have gone beyond this limit, explanations are given in the Glossary, which also explains some allusions that may be unfamiliar to the student. As to the comprehension questions, the first ten require a scanning of the text to find the answer; the second ten are more concerned with making deductions from the text, and often invite the student to offer an opinion with reasons. There is a range of exercise types to provide interest and variety. In B and C, the answers can be found in the story itself. The section called 'Wordgame' contains some light-hearted exercises to practise some of the vocabulary from the story. For the discussion questions, students should, if possible, work in pairs or small groups.

Introduction

I have received many letters from students (and their teachers) from countries far and near – Japan, Turkey, Germany, Italy, and so on – containing comments about my earlier stories, both complimentary and critical, which have encouraged me greatly. I thank them all, and hope I may hear from them (or their successors) when they use the present book. I am grateful to Lâle Çolakoğlu for her help, and also for explaining about soapmaking in Altınoluk. My thanks go also to my daughter, Sarah, for checking the manuscript and for keeping me in touch with reality.

Best Friends

Clearly there was nobody at home: those newspapers sticking out of the letterbox are a sure sign that the owners are away.

'Come on! Let's break in!'

'I don't think we should. It's not like stealing apples.'

5 'Are you afraid? Chicken!'

'Who's chicken? I'll show you.'

Being taller than Ginger, Deggy was able to reach up and open the window. The boys climbed in and looked around. Then they heard the screech of breaks as a car pulled up outside
10 the house. They ran as fast as they could. Ginger got away, but Deggy tripped and fell. The policeman grabbed Deggy by the collar and took him to the police station. They questioned him for hours and hours. They wanted to know the other boy's name, but he didn't tell them.

15 Meanwhile, Ginger sat at home, terrified. He expected at any moment to hear policemen knocking on his door. But he needn't have worried. His friend Deggy said nothing. He was sent to prison for a year. When he got out, he knew that his parents did not want him, so he decided to go and see his old friend,
20 Ginger. Ginger had not visited him in prison. Perhaps his parents had told him not to.

Deggy did not recognise the woman who opened the door.

'Oh, they don't live here any more. I think they moved to Birmingham, but I am not sure. Sorry.'

25

The platform was crowded. It was the rush hour, and a crowd of business men and women were waiting for the train to take them back to their comfortable homes in the suburbs. Among the waiting passengers was a tall man in an expensive overcoat.
30 He had the fat face of a man who lives well and eats only the

4

best food. He was standing under the notice that said 'Beware of Pickpockets'. A slim red-haired man was moving quickly through the crowd. He worked his way over to the tall well-fed man, bumped into him and then slipped away quickly. Unfortunately for him, a railway policeman had seen the whole thing. He grabbed the slim man by the collar, and dragged him to where the tall man was standing.

'Excuse me, sir,' the policeman said, 'but would you be good enough to check your pockets.'

'Good heavens! My wallet! I can't find my wallet.'

The policeman pulled the slim man up by his collar. 'Come on, let's have it!'

The pickpocket took the wallet out and handed it over to the policeman.

'Is this your wallet, sir?'

'Yes, it is! Look. Those are my initials.'

He looked down at the thief, his eyes filled with disgust. At that moment, despite the fact that he had not seen him in twenty-five years, he recognised his childhood friend, Ginger, the one he had been with when they had broken into a house and the police had come and . . .

Ginger kept his eyes fixed on the ground. He had no interest in staring into the face of the man he had just tried to rob.

'Do you want to press charges against this man, sir?' the policeman asked. There was a moment's silence.

'Of course, officer,' Deggy said. 'We must teach these thieves a lesson.'

The pickpocket shrugged his shoulders. He didn't even hate the businessman. That's the way the world is, he thought to himself as the policeman took him away. Meanwhile, Deggy, the successful businessman, had boarded his train, satisfied that he had done his duty as a good citizen.

A Walk on the Beach

Little Yosef had his new sailor suit on. It was blue and white
and had a little sailor hat to match. It was not the sort of present
a boy would choose for his sixth birthday, but it was better than
nothing. He looked up at the grown-ups and smiled. Mother
5 looked down at him and felt proud. Father looked down at him
and felt proud. Grandma, who was staying with them for a week
or two, looked down at him and said: 'I'll take him for a walk
along the beach.'

'Oh no!' thought Mother. 'Oh no!' thought Father. Little
10 Yosef liked the idea and he smiled again. Grandma waited.

'Perhaps it isn't a very good idea,' said Father.

'Why don't you just take him for a walk in the garden?' said
Mother, thinking that it was much safer.

'Nonsense,' said Grandma. 'Yosef and I will be all right,
15 won't we, Yossi?'

The child smiled again. He liked his grandma and he liked
going to the beach. He liked to watch the huge waves coming
in off the sea.

Father thought of those huge waves and shook his head.
20 Grandma was getting old and careless. It wasn't a good idea at
all.

'Come on, Yossi! Off we go!' said Grandma.

'Just don't let go of his hand!' said Mother.

'I won't!'

25 'Promise!' said Father.

'Don't make such a fuss!' said Grandma.

As soon as they were on the beach, little Yosef managed to get
away from Grandma and went to stand right by the water's
30 edge to watch the waves. Grandma looked up at the sky. It was

a lovely day, sunny and windless. The sea was calm, thank goodness. She sat down on the sand and watched her little Yossi.

'Be careful, darling!' she shouted. 'Don't go too near the water.'

He turned and smiled at her. Just at that moment, out of nowhere, a huge wave crashed on the beach. A really huge wave. When it flowed back into the sea, Yosef had disappeared. The wave had swept him out to sea. Grandma ran to the water's edge, screaming.

'Oh Lord! What has happened? Oh Lord! Oh no! Please bring little Yossi back!'

For the first time in many years, Grandma prayed. She prayed to all the gods she could think of. She prayed to Wodan and Tanrı and Osiris. Then she prayed to the Great Spirit and to several other gods whose names she couldn't quite remember.

In all her prayers, she promised to be good, to be a perfect grandmother, a perfect citizen, anything as long as they would send her Yossi back to her. She had never felt so bad in all her life. Yossi's parents were right. She was not to be trusted any more.

At that moment, another huge wave, even bigger than the first one, crashed on the beach. She looked down. There was little Yosef, sitting on the sand, pale and wet, but otherwise all right. He looked up at his grandma and smiled.

She picked him up, held him tight, covered him with kisses, and thanked all the gods for bringing her little grandson back to her. She put him down and began to tidy him up in that fussy way that grandmothers have. She ran her fingers through his hair. And then she stopped suddenly. Leaving the little boy on the sand, she went to the water's edge. Her face was red with anger. She looked up into the sky and shouted as loudly as she could: 'Where's his hat?'

Family Fortune

In 1840, times were hard for Bentley Harcourt. He had a farm in Yorkshire, but it didn't make money. He wanted to marry, but decided to wait until better times came along. Better times did not come along. One day, he saw a newspaper article about the American West. It sounded like the land of milk and honey. He thought about it. He had no family. Nobody cared if he lived or died. Why not make a new life in the New World? He sold his farm and emigrated to America. After a year of drifting, he found himself in Texas. He loved it. He loved the fact that you could travel for days and not meet another soul. He used his savings to buy some land. That year, he died.

In 1910, an oil company moved on to his land and found oil. They took millions of barrels of oil out of the ground. All the profits due to the owner of the land were paid into a bank account in Houston, where they waited for a relative to claim them. The money sat in the bank for years. By 1975, the amount stood at two billion dollars.

In 1975, in Bradford, England, a man called David Kingsley took up a new hobby – tracing his family tree. He studied church records, visited museums, checked every reference to families called Kingsley. He also checked on his mother's family. They were called Harcourt. He discovered one day that his mother's great-great-uncle, a man with the splendid name of Bentley Harcourt, had sailed from Liverpool to America on the *SS Enterprise*.

In the same year, shortly after learning about his great-great-uncle, Kingsley read a magazine article about a fortune that lay unclaimed in a Texas bank. The article told the story of a lonely immigrant called Bentley Harcourt, and about how he had died shortly after buying his dream ranch in Texas. The magazine offered to pay the legal expenses of anyone who could claim to be a descendant and who might be entitled to the fortune. Kingsley read the story with mounting excitement. Surely this must be the same Bentley Harcourt that he had come across during his research into his family tree? He talked the matter over with his wife and then wrote to the magazine.   35

As it turned out, Kingsley was not the only one who claimed to be a descendant. By the end of 1997, over sixty people were claiming they were entitled to the fortune. The arguments, the quarrels and the court cases went on and on and on. In the end,   40
Kingsley did not get the $2bn, but, funnily enough, he didn't mind. He had found something much more important. He had a great-great-uncle called Bentley Harcourt, there was no doubt about that. But, amazingly, his was a *different* Bentley Harcourt. It seemed impossible that there could be two people with such   45
an unusual name, but it was true. This Bentley Harcourt had settled in Orange County, California and had made his fortune in fish canning. He married a hardworking Swedish girl, and they had thirteen children. David Kingsley had found a different treasure: a branch of his family across the Atlantic. The two   50
families wrote to each other. Later, they visited each other. They became the best of friends.

And the fortune of the other Bentley Harcourt? It is still unclaimed. As I write this, the sum stands at $2.3 billion. This may be a good moment to start tracing your family tree.   55

A Free Lunch

'Good morning, gentlemen. I am Cardosa, at your service!'

The group he was addressing were all women, but that did not bother Cardosa. He was proud of the English he had learned as a youngster. He spoked rapidly, smiling all the time as he did so. Unfortunately, he rarely understood what was said to him, but this did not bother him either.

The women stared at him, not sure if he was an official or a madman.

'Welcome to Lubango. Welcome to the Grand Hotel. Anything you want, ask Cardosa!'

The leader of the group decided he must be an official. 'We are here for the conference, Comrade er . . .'

'Cardosa. C-A-R-D-O-S-A. I am an Angolan citizen. Welcome!'

She looked at him. He was clearly a European, probably one of those Portuguese who had stayed on after Independence. 'We are here for the conference.'

'Ah yes, a beautiful country,' said Cardosa with another broad smile.

The women were from North Korea and weren't confident of their English. They didn't know if they had not understood him, or if he did not understand them.

'North Korea,' said the leader uncertainly. 'We have come for the Trade Union Congress.'

Cardosa smiled again. He recognised the word 'congress'; it was almost the same word in Portuguese. 'Ah yes, the Congress! Please follow me, gentlemen.'

The women looked at each other and then at Cardosa. He spread his arms out. 'Do not worry! I know the way. I will take you to the conference room.' He led the way and the women, having no better alternative, followed him. He kept up a conversation over his shoulder as he walked. 'Pleased to meet you. How are you? Anything you need? A taxi, cigarettes, eat, drink . . . just ask Cardosa.'

'We are the North Korean delegation,' the leader said. 'Who are you?'

'I am very well,' replied Cardosa.

'Are you our guide?'

He looked at his watch. It no longer worked, but it looked good on his wrist. 'Eight-thirty!' he said confidently. The leader looked at her colleagues and shook her head.

He showed the delegates into the conference room and bowed low. 'Goodbye. See you later, er, comrades.'

When they came out at the end of the morning session, Cardosa was waiting for them. 'Good! You have talked, now you must eat. Follow me.' As he led them towards the dining-room, the leader tried again.

'Are you a government official, Comrade Cardosa?'

'Very good. Yes, the food here is very good. You will enjoy it!'

He sat next to the leader at the long dining-table which had been laid specially for them.

'This', he said, holding up something grey on the end of his fork, 'is a local speciality, *bacalhau*. Codfish.' He spoke as if he had personally caught it that morning just for them.

'It looks very good,' said the leader.

'I do, too,' he said. The leader shook her head again. She was glad when the lunch was over. It was a good lunch, though, and Cardosa went for a sleep in his taxi when the women went back to their conference.

A couple of weeks later, a delegation of Cuban women arrived in Lubango for the Women's Health Congress. As they walked into the hotel on the first morning, a funny little man came to greet them, a big smile on his face.

'Good morning, gentlemen. I am Cardosa, at your service!'

His taxi business made very little money, but Cardosa certainly knew how to get a free lunch.

Departures

'I found it lying on the balcony. I could see that it was still alive. I've got it in a box.'

'Hmm.'

'The thing is, Paul, I've no idea what to do with it, but I don't want to let it die.'

'I see. Do you know what species it is, Renos?'

'I don't know. It's black with a white throat. Long wings.'

Oh no! Paul thought. *A swift! It is almost impossible to feed a baby swift. It's sure to die.* Aloud he said: 'Sounds like a swift. Difficult.'

'Look, I'm sorry to bother you but I don't know anyone in Greece who is interested in birds.'

Yes, thought Paul, *it does seem crazy for a man in Athens to be phoning someone in London about a baby bird.* Aloud he said: 'Why don't you put it back in the nest?'

'I've looked and I can't find the nest. What shall I do?'

Paul thought to himself: *Let it die*, but he knew he couldn't say that. 'Keep it warm and feed it with, er, with tiny pieces of cat food.'

'How do I get the food down its throat? How often should I feed it? Does it need water too?'

Paul answered Renos's questions as best he could.

'Thanks a lot, Paul. I'll phone you again to let you know how things are going.'

'Best of luck, Renos.'

Maryjean looked at the skinny thing in the box.

'What an ugly bird. What is it?'

'It's a swift. I found it on the balcony. I'm trying to feed it.'

Maryjean shrugged her shoulders. 'A waste of time, if you ask me.'

She watched the loving way in which Renos held the tiny bird in his hand while he fed it. She suddenly felt angry again, the same anger that she had felt the other night. 'I'm going.'

'What? I thought we were going out together this evening.'

'Forget it. I can see you're *much* too busy.' 35

The door slammed as she left. He fed the swift and thought about Maryjean. He was fond of Maryjean, but did he really love her? And did she really love him? They seemed to fight a lot, but maybe that was a sign that they did love each other. They had met in July. She had come over from the States to 40 spend the summer studying Ancient Greek architecture. She had talked about staying on after the summer . . . The bird was having difficulty in swallowing the cat meat.

'Hello, Paul. It's me again.' 45

'Hello, Renos, how's the bird?'

'Not good. It won't eat. It spends most of its time sleeping.'

'Well, don't be upset if the bird doesn't make it. Swifts eat insects, and that makes them difficult to feed. Now, if it ate seeds like a goldfinch, say . . .' 50

'It's not a goldfinch!' Renos retorted. 'Sorry, Paul. Look, I really need your help.'

'Try feeding it on fish soaked in milk.'

Maryjean came round three days later. Renos was still nursing the tiny bird. 55

'I'm going, Renos. I've had enough.'

'What?' He had hardly noticed her standing there. The door slammed as she left.

'Paul? Bad news, I'm afraid. It died this morning.' 60

'Sorry.'

'Thanks for your help anyway.'

He went out on to the balcony and looked up into the evening sky. There were swifts flying round everywhere. Above them, high in the sky, a Boeing 747 was winging its way west. In seat 65 14D, an American student of Ancient Greek architecture was settling down for her return flight to New York.

Happy Days

Harry and Christopher stood on the stage and looked at their teacher.

'Get on with it,' Amanda Pratt said.

Harry shouted his lines: *'I am Robin Hood! I steal from the rich and give to the poor! Give me your money!'*

Christopher, who was playing the rich merchant, pointed at Harry's head. 'Please, Mrs Pratt, Harry's wearing my hat! He's Robin Hood and Robin Hood always wore a *green* hat and Harry's wearing my *red* hat.'

The teacher looked at Christopher, who was wearing a green hat. It was very confusing. 'It doesn't matter, Christopher. Just say your lines.'

Christopher stood and stared at her. She knew *nothing* about Robin Hood.

'But Robin Hood always wore a *green* hat. *Everyone* knows that.'

'Oh, very well, then. Harry, give Christopher his red hat, and you put on the green one.'

'But', said Harry, 'this isn't Christopher's red hat. This is David's red hat.'

'So, which hat is David wearing?'

Harry spoke to her as if to a small child.

'David doesn't *need* a hat. He plays Friar Tuck. Friar Tuck doesn't wear a hat'.

At that moment, the Head came into the Hall.

'Ah, Mrs Pratt, how's the school play going? Shall we be ready on the night? Only three days to go, hmm?'

With these children, she thought, we'll never be ready: not in three days, three months or three centuries. 'Yes, Headmaster,' she replied, crossing her fingers. 'We shall be ready on the night. All right, children. Let's start again.'

The children all left the stage except for Christopher, the rich

14

merchant about to be robbed by Robin Hood. Christopher shuffled across the stage making a noise like a railway engine going up a hill: *'Choo-choo-choo-choo-choo . . .'* Amanda hoped that the Headmaster would not notice. Harry, alias Robin Hood, jumped out and spoke his line: *'I am Robin Hood! I steal from the rich and give to the poor! Give me your money!'*

The Headmaster coughed.

'Ahem! Excuse me, Mrs Pratt, but why is Robin Hood wearing a *red* hat?' he asked. 'Everyone knows that Robin Hood always wore *green*.' He came up and whispered in her ear. 'These small details are important, Amanda.'

Back in the teachers' room, Amanda sat down, a cup of coffee in her shaking hand.

'Hi, Amanda! How's the play going?'

'It's very kind of you to ask, Julie, but let's talk about something else.'

'Sorry. What's the problem?'

'The problem, Julie, is called Christopher Price. And Harry Jones. And David Glossop. And all the rest of the little . . .'

'Yes, school would be wonderful without children, wouldn't it?'

The two women stayed silent for a moment. What a wonderful idea! A school with only teachers in it.

The next afternoon, Amanda was again in the Hall. Christopher shuffled across the stage: *'Choo-choo-choo-choo-choo . . .'*

'Christopher, why are you making that ridiculous noise? You are supposed to be riding through Sherwood Forest on a horse.'

Christopher stared at her. 'I know that!' he said indignantly. 'But I don't know how to make a noise like a horse, so I am making a noise like a train instead.'

He shook his head. Teachers understood *nothing*. What was the point of teachers, anyway? School would be fine if there weren't any teachers. What a wonderful idea? A school with only children in it.

A Load of Old Rubbish

Miss Darby was one of those people who never threw anything away. *'You never know when you might need it,'* was one of her favourite sayings. She lived alone in a large Victorian house across the road from us. Although I never went into her house, I knew it was full of valuable things: antique furniture, Persian carpets and so on. She loved art; every inch of her walls was taken up by paintings. I can remember my father saying that she was 'a Staffordshire Darby'. I had no idea what he meant. I found out years later that the Darby family had made their money from coalmining in the county of Staffordshire. We children used to make up stories about her. My sister Alice, who was a romantic, whispered to us: 'She was engaged to be married, but her fiancé was killed in the Great War. Now she lives alone, broken-hearted.'

My brother Alan, who was just coming into adolescence, had another idea: 'They say she's a white witch and she can cure spots just by staring at them.'

With my wild imagination, I had my own story about Miss Darby: 'She's got six children. She keeps them locked in a dark cellar.'

She rarely went out, and nobody came to visit her. Nobody, that is, except for Mrs Triggs, her housekeeper. Mrs Triggs was a friend of my mother's and a great gossip. One day I heard her saying how Miss Darby never threw anything away.

'Bundles of newspapers! Hundreds of them, everywhere! I try to throw them out, but she just goes out and brings them back into the house. I give up!'

'Have another cup of tea, Mrs Triggs.'

It was only when she died that we found out that Miss Darby had two nephews. They inherited everything: her money, and the house and all its contents. The nephews came across to say hello, and my mother made them a cup of tea.

'Are you thinking of moving into the house?' my mother asked politely.

'Good heavens, no! We live in Stafford. No, we've just come 35 down to empty the house.'

'I believe your aunt has . . . had . . . a lot of nice things.'

The nephews nodded. They described what was in the house. It sounded like Aladdin's Cave.

Over the next few days, we children watched them coming 40 and going, and wished we could join in. Most of the stuff was taken away in a huge furniture van. They also had a smaller van which took away all the rubbish that their aunt had refused to get rid of, mostly great bundles of newspapers. My brother Alan asked the nephews if he could have one of the bundles of 45 newspapers. We read the headline on the top newspaper: 'RUSSIAN TANKS ROLL INTO BUDAPEST'. It was dated 10 November 1956! Alan took out his penknife and cut the string with which the bundle was tied. We spread the newspapers out, curious to read about things that had happened over fifty years ago. 50

'What's this?' said Alice, holding something she had found inside the top newspaper.

'Here's another!' said Alan, opening the second newspaper in the bundle.

'And another! And another!' I shouted, as I worked my way 55 through the newspapers.

'What are they? They look like paintings without frames.'

This bundle alone contained twenty-five beautiful paintings. We later learned that they were originals, worth at least £500 each. By the time the nephews learned of our discovery, they 60 had already thrown out most of the hundreds of bundles of newspapers.

Rent Free

'Don't fall in!'

'Ignore him,' Marja whispered to Rosemary. 'He's just trying to get friendly with us.'

'Hi! I'm Tov,' said the young man. 'Look, there's the island of Crete. Have you been to Crete before?'

'No, this is our first time. What about you?'

'Oh, I've been there several times. How long will you stay on Crete?'

'It depends,' said Rosemary. 'We're broke, but if we could get a job and earn some money . . .'

'Ah!' said Tov. 'I think I can help you.'

That night, Rosemary and Marja stayed in Heraklion. Tov promised to call for them next morning.

'Grape picking! It sounds terrible!' said Marja. 'And I don't trust your friend Tov.'

'He's worked in the vineyard, he knows the farmer, he can arrange everything. I think we've been very lucky. We don't speak a word of Greek. Could we find work without Tov's help?'

Tov met them next morning and they all got on to an old bus which took them into the mountains above Heraklion. Eventually, they came to a valley with vineyards everywhere.

'Look! That's old Loizou's house!'

The farmer – 'old Loizou' – and his wife greeted Tov and the girls and offered them coffee. The old couple could only speak Greek. Tov translated. Loizou and his wife smiled and nodded at the girls. The conversation continued. When Rosemary heard the word 'drachma', she guessed they were talking about the work.

'It's all arranged,' said Tov at last. 'You will work for Mr Loizou. I have told him that you will work here for two weeks. He will pay you at the end of the time.'

'Where shall we stay?'

'Ah yes, I nearly forgot. There isn't anywhere for you to sleep here at the farm. You can sleep in a barn at the other end of the village.'

'Whose barn?'

'It belongs to Mr Loizou's brother. I slept there when I was grape picking last year. It's very comfortable.' Next morning, as he was leaving, Tov said: 'Goodbye! All the best!'

'Goodbye, Tov. And thanks.'

'Oh yes, there's something I forgot to mention . . .' he began, but at that moment, Loizou called to him. After he had left, Marja said: 'I wonder what he was going to tell us?'

The fortnight went by quickly and the girls, suntanned and happy, went on Friday night to see old Loizou to collect their money and to say goodbye. They wanted to make an early start next morning to do some sightseeing in the rest of the island. Loizou gave them their money and then indicated with hand gestures that they were to eat with him and his family that evening. And what a wonderful evening it was! *Mezes* of every kind, followed by fruit and pastries.

All the Loizous were there. Old Loizou's son, Andreas, arrived halfway through the evening, just back from his first year at university in Athens. 'How do you like grape picking?' he asked in his best English.

'Hard work. It was fun, but we're glad it's over.'

The boy looked at them, puzzled.

'Over? But you have another week to do yet. For my uncle.'

'Your uncle? What do you mean?'

He explained about the 'rent' for staying in the barn. They had to pick grapes for Loizou's brother for one week without pay. Tov had forgotten to tell them.

Next morning, before dawn, while everyone was sleeping, the two girls climbed out of a window at the back of the barn and crept away down the mountain to Heraklion. They did not speak. They could not look at each other.

The Perfect Woman

You know how it is when men get together. They talk about impossible dreams: 'If I won the lottery, I would . . .', 'If I had plenty of money, I would . . .' Well, I was just like all the other men who used to sit in the coffee house talking nonsense. But
5 I never told anyone about my dream. I was afraid they would laugh if they knew. And then, believe it or not, one day I found that I was indeed rich. My aunt Camilla died and left everything to me. She had some valuable paintings. I sold them, and set off round the world in search of . . . the perfect woman. You
10 see, I had always wanted to get married but I had never been able to find a woman that I really loved. I decided that it was better not to make do with second best, but to wait and hope that one day I would meet the woman of my dreams.

I first went to America. I must have visited every state, but I
15 did not find what I was looking for. The women I met were either too thin or too fat, too quiet or too noisy, too fair or too dark. So I set off for Australia. I didn't stay there very long. Most of the women I met were much too, well, self-confident. They made me feel uncomfortable. Then I went to Thailand.
20 The women there were lovely, but much too shy, and anyway I prefer taller women. Finally, I found myself back in my own country. I was sad. How was it possible to meet so many women and not find one that suited me?

Well, you can guess what happened. In my own country, I
25 found the woman I was looking for! Funnily enough, she lived near me, and I was amazed that I had not noticed her before. We met in the local supermarket. She dropped her purse. I picked it up and gave it to her. She smiled at me and said thank you, and I knew at that moment that she was the woman for
30 me. But I wanted to be very careful. I didn't want to say or do

anything that might frighten her away. So I just made small talk as we walked back to the car park.

Back home, I planned my campaign to win her heart. After a few more meetings, I finally invited her to have dinner with me. She accepted. 35

I am not a very good cook, but I believe that if you lay the table properly, nobody will notice the food. I went out and bought an expensive tablecloth and some silver knives and forks. I laid the table, put a huge bowl of flowers in the middle, then stood back and admired the result. As a finishing touch, I put 40 two silver candlesticks on the table. A perfect table for a perfect woman.

Everything went well during dinner. She admired the flowers and the candlesticks. She complimented me on my cooking (she was just being kind, of course) and the conversation flowed 45 easily. Finally, as we sat drinking coffee, I told her about my search.

'. . . so, when my aunt Camilla left me well off, I decided to set off round the world in search of the perfect woman.'

'That is amazing!' she exclaimed. 'I've just come into a lot of 50 money, too, and I have decided to set off round the world in search of the perfect man. I hope I find him.'

I tried to smile, but it wasn't easy.

Cabbage White

'So you're looking for work, And who are you?'

'I'm Sarah. I'm twelve. This is my brother Jamie; he's eleven.'

'Shouldn't you be at school?'

5 'We're on holiday. And we would like to earn some money.'

The man lifted his hat and scratched his bald head. 'All right. Let's see. Do you know what a Cabbage White is?

'It is a beautiful white butterfly that lays its eggs on cabbages. And those eggs change into caterpillars. And do you know what 10 the caterpillars do?'

'They eat the cabbage leaves!' shouted Jamie.

'Well done, Jamie! So, I want you to check every single cabbage in the garden and remove all the caterpillars.'

'Er . . . how?'

15 'You pick them off the leaves and put them in a bucket.'

'How much will you pay us?'

'Let's see how you get on, first. I'll be in the greenhouse. Get started and I'll see you later.'

Shortly, armed with a bucket each, the children approached 20 the cabbage patch. It was huge. 'There must a *million* cabbages here!' Jamie said.

'At least!' Sarah said. 'And if there are ten caterpillars on each cabbage, that makes, er, a billion caterpillars!'

Sarah stood open-mouthed. Jamie wondered about her arith- 25 metic, but knew better than to argue.

They started on the first row of cabbages. It was a horrible business. The caterpillars wriggled as they were picked up. It took the two children ages to finish the first row, and already they couldn't see the bottom of their buckets for caterpillars. 30 And all around them, the air was filled with Cabbage White

22

butterflies. The insects seemed to be making fun of them. They seemed to be saying: 'We don't care if you kill our caterpillars. We can lay millions more eggs.'

Sarah struck out at a butterfly. She missed, of course. She watched it fly happily away. Then she had an idea, as brilliant in its way as Einstein coming up with $e = mc^2$.

'Jamie, caterpillars come from eggs, right?'

He nodded.

'And where do the eggs come from?'

'The butterflies lay them.'

'Right. So', she reasoned, 'if we get rid of the butterflies, there won't be any more eggs or caterpillars.'

'Right.' Jamie decided to agree, just in case she had gone mad.

'So, why don't we just get rid of the butterflies!'

'How?'

Nearby, there were beans climbing up bamboo poles. Sarah removed two poles. Two bean plants died. She handed one of the poles to Jamie, and then rushed into the cabbage patch, swinging her pole round and round trying to hit the butterflies. This seemed to Jamie like a good game, so he followed her. It is not easy to hit flying butterflies, but it is not difficult to hit them when they settle on cabbages. Soon the ground was covered with dead butterflies. Sarah and Jamie fought on until they were exhausted. Then they stood back to admire their work. There were hardly any butterflies left. There were hardly any cabbages left, either. It is difficult to hit a butterfly on a cabbage without hitting the cabbage too. The cabbage patch looked like a battlefield. Not a cabbage was left standing. The children looked at each other. Without a word, they put down the bamboo poles and tiptoed out of the garden.

'He knows our names,' Jamie said.

'But he doesn't know where we live,' Sarah said.

'Thank goodness,' they both said.

The Pony and the Donkey

Rochelle and Emma were mad about horses. They both lived near a farm, and visited the farmer's horses whenever they could. Neither of them had ever been on a horse, but each one dreamed of the day when she would have her own pony to ride. When
5 the annual Children's Poetry Competition came round, they stared at the notice in disbelief. Instead of the usual boring prizes – a book, a visit to the museum, etc – the prize this year was a day's ponytrekking!

'Let's enter, shall we, Emma?'

10 'What do you mean, Rochelle? Write a poem? English is my worst subject.'

'Same here. But it's worth trying, Em. Just think, a whole day's ponytrekking!'

'But what'll we write about?'

15 'Well, I shall write a poem about a pony!'

'We can't *both* write about the same thing, can we, Rochelle?'

'Well, I tell you what. You write about a pony, and I'll write about a . . .' She couldn't think of anything. Emma came to her
20 rescue.

'What about a donkey, Rochelle?'

'Don't be stupid, Emma. I can't stand donkeys. Stupid animals.'

'All right, Rochelle I tell you what: you write about a pony,
25 and I'll write about a donkey.'

They sent for entry forms and set to work. For days, they worked on their poems, seeking the right words, trying to find rhymes, scratching their heads. Finally they both had something to send off. Emma went round to Rochelle's house.

30 'Come on, Rochelle, let me hear yours.'

'All right, but only if you'll let me hear yours, Em. I can't imagine what you found to say about a donkey!'

'Go on. You first.'

Rochelle cleared her throat and began to read aloud. *'Pretty little pony: Pretty little pony with a brand new saddle, Trotting through the traffic with its head held high . . .'* 35

Emma listened to the end and said how good it was. Then it was her turn.

'The donkey: My head is too big and my ears are too long, My legs are too short, and my tail is all wrong . . .' 40

When she had heard the whole of Emma's poem about the donkey, Rochelle said: 'Yours is bound to win. It's brilliant!'

'No,' said Emma. 'Yours is much better. I bet you win.' For the first time, the two girls realised that only one of them could win. It made them think. They left the poems and entry forms 45 for Rochelle's mother to put into envelopes and post, and went out to play.

The winner got a letter: *'Congratulations! Your poem has won first prize in this year's Children's Poetry Competition. It will be published in next week's* Hampshire Gazette. *Please come to Sopley* 50 *Stables at 9 am on Saturday 20 June . . .'*

Rochelle had a wonderful day at Sopley. She only wished Emma could have been there, too. In fact, Emma had gone on holiday with her parents, and didn't even know that Rochelle had won the poetry prize. There was still one more treat for 55 Rochelle: seeing her poem printed in the local newspaper. When the paper arrived, she leafed through the pages impatiently. Inside, there was a report of the competition and the winning poem. It began:

'My head is too big and my ears are too long . . .' 60

It wasn't her poem, it was Emma's poem! Rochelle couldn't understand it. The entry forms and the poems must have got mixed up when her mother put them in the envelopes. How could she face Emma? What would she say? 'Emma, your poem was best, but I was the one who went ponytrekking.' For a 65 while, Rochelle felt really bad. Then she said to herself: 'Stupid judges! Fancy preferring a stupid poem about a stupid donkey!'

Say That Again

'*At that moment, I wished the ground would open and swallow me up.*' You must have had moments like that. You say to a woman at a party: 'Who is that ugly man over there?' and she replies: 'He is my son'. Or you sound your horn angrily at a motorist who has done something stupid, and when he turns to stare at you, you realise that it is your boss. No? You have never experienced a moment like that? Then you have been lucky. Unlike poor Arthur Bridge.

Wolfsburg in Germany is the home of Volkswagen. It is also where trainees from all over the world are sent to study chemistry in Dr Schumann's *Chemisches Institut*. Some years ago, the Libyan government asked a group of German companies to build a chemical plant at Abu Kammash. The German companies also agreed to train several hundred young Libyans. This is how, one year, Dr Schumann's institute came to have a large group of Libyan trainees.

Arthur Bridge, a British chemical engineer working in Tripoli, was asked to visit the Wolfsburg trainees to report on their progress. His visit was taken very seriously not only by Dr Schumann, but also by the companies who were building Abu Kammash. For Arthur's visit, there were six company representatives in Wolfsburg that day.

That evening, Arthur and Dr Schumann and the representatives went into Hannover for dinner. Conversation was about the trainees and about Abu Kammash. But, as the evening wore on, conversation became more and more difficult. Silence fell on the company. Arthur, feeling that someone should try to keep the conversation going, turned to the man sitting next to him, a bald man with glasses that kept slipping down his nose.

'This wine is excellent, but I must admit that I know nothing about German wines. All these different labels: *Tafelwein, Mit Prädikat, Spätauslese,* and so on. What do they mean?'

The man, equally keen to break the embarrassing silence, gave Arthur a detailed explanation of the different grades of German wine. Arthur nodded frequently, but, to tell the truth, his German was not very good (except when he was talking about chemical engineering) and he understood very little. Anyway, it didn't matter, because the evening ended well. Everyone said goodnight, and Arthur went back to his hotel, able to relax at last.

He went back to Tripoli to rejoin his company, and thought no more about his German trip. The trainees stayed on in Wolfsburg, the plant in Abu Kammash neared completion. Months went by. One day, Arthur was asked to visit the trainees again. When he arrived at the Schumann Institute, he vaguely remembered his first visit. *The sooner this is over, the better,* he thought.

That evening, he found himself in a restaurant in Hannover with Dr Schumann and a number of company representatives, whose faces he could scarcely recognise. The evening dragged on. Once the usual topics – training and Abu Kammash – had been exhausted, conversation died. Arthur tried to find something else to talk about. He turned to the man sitting next to him and said: 'This wine is excellent, but I must admit that I know nothing about German wines. All these different labels: *Tafelwein, Mit Prädikat, Spätauslese,* and so on. What do they mean?'

The man pushed his glasses back up his nose. Spacing his words out as if he were speaking to an idiot, the man said to Arthur:

'Herr – Bridge, – you – asked – me – exactly – the – same – question – nine – months – ago . . .'

Are you *sure* you have never had a moment like that?

April Fool

'Where's my blue file?'

'Blue file?' said Elizabeth's father. 'Was that *your* blue file? Sorry, Elizabeth, I threw it away.'

Elizabeth's face fell. 'But, Dad, it had all my French notes in
5 it! I've got a French examination tomorrow.'

'Maybe it's still in the dustbin.'

Elizabeth went and looked in the dustbin. Nothing. When she went back into the kitchen, the blue file was on the table.

'April Fool!' shouted her father, laughing.

10 William, Elizabeth's brother, looked up. He didn't think it was very funny.

'Well', said Father, 'I must be off to work. Have a nice day, children. Oh, and William: take off that shirt. It's got a stain on it.'

15 William looked down. There was no stain on it.

'April Fool!' shouted Father.

Elizabeth and William left the house together. Their mother watched them through the kitchen window as they walked down the road. They had their heads together.

20

Several weeks later, the family were having breakfast when the post arrived.

'One for you, Elizabeth,' Father said. 'From the London Examinations Board. Hmm, must be important.'

25 Elizabeth picked up the envelope and rushed upstairs with it.

'What's the matter with her?' asked Father.

'I think they are her examination results,' her mother said.

Elizabeth came down a few minutes later and sat silently at the table.

30 'Well?' said her mother.

Elizabeth looked at her father. 'I've passed in every subject, except French,' she said.

'Well done, Elizabeth!' said her mother.

Elizabeth waited for a word of praise from her father, but none came.

'What happened with your French then?' he said. 'I got an A in French when I was at school. You're just no good at languages.'

Elizabeth ran upstairs. Her mother shook her head.

'Where are you going, Elizabeth?' her father asked one Sunday morning.

'I'm having private lessons in French.'

'Why?'

'I need French to get into university, Dad.'

'Well, you'll never pass. It's a waste of time and money if you ask me.'

April the first came round again. This time, William and Elizabeth were ready to pay their father back for the tricks he had played on them. He loved his garden, and he was very proud of his lawn. So, early on April the first, before their parents were up, William and Elizabeth went into the garden and put several small piles of earth on the lawn. From a distance, the piles of earth looked like molehills. Later, when everyone was seated at the breakfast table, William looked out of the window and asked: 'What's that on the lawn?'

Father saw the 'molehills' and went red with anger. Moles had dug up his lawn! He began to swear.

'April Fool, Dad!' shouted the children, laughing.

Their father turned on them angrily. 'Stupid children! Go and clean up the mess.

'It was only a joke, Dad,' began William. 'We . . .'

'Get out and clear up that mess! Every bit!'

Some weeks later, an official-looking envelope dropped through the letterbox. Elizabeth opened it.

'Mummy! I've passed my French!'

'Oh, that's wonderful, Elizabeth! Your father will be pleased.'

Elizabeth looked away. 'Mummy, don't tell him. I don't want him to know that I passed my French. Ever.'

Soap

What a good year it was for olives! There was just enough rain in spring and just enough sunshine in summer. The olives ripened perfectly in the warm autumn sun. Osman knew, when he went to check his olive trees, that he was going to have the best crop of olives ever. Sitting in her chair in the corner, Osman's daughter Zeynep knew, from the way her father winked at her, that the olive crop would be a good one. She knew that there would be enough money to buy her a white silk dress for her twelfth birthday party, after the harvest.

Zeynep looked at herself in every mirror. It was a beautiful dress, and she studied herself from every angle. In the front garden, family, friends and neighbours were sitting round, chatting and sipping cool drinks while they waited for the party to begin. The tables in the garden were heaped with good food. All that was missing was the Birthday Girl. At the back of the house, Zeynep, the Birthday Girl, wanted to be alone for a while. She wanted to believe she looked beautiful in her dress, before she went into the garden. One moment she felt like a filmstar, and the next she was worried that the people might not take any notice of her at all.

Meanwhile, the guests chatted on about this and that. Of course, the most important topic of conversation was the excellent olive harvest, the best that anyone in Altınoluk could remember.

'*Hamd olsun!* We have had olives the size of peaches this year!'

'The first pressing produced the best olive oil I have ever seen!'

'Thick and beautiful, like liquid gold!'

'*Elhamdulillah!* Praise be to God!'

'So, Osman *bey*, what about the soap?'

Osman grinned. 'We shall make enough soap to wash all the feet in Altınoluk a thousand times over.'

'Waste not, want not, eh, Osman *bey*?'

Round at the back of the house was the huge container in which the soap was made from the last pressings of the olives, skins and stones and all. The container itself was about half the size of a football pitch. It had a low wooden wall all round it to keep in the liquid. The children loved to walk along the top of the narrow wall, pretending they were walking a circus tightrope. They loved to skip or to hop. They liked the feeling of danger. They might slip or fall into the horrible soup at any moment.

Everyone stopped talking when they heard the scream. For a moment, nobody reacted. When they heard a second scream, they all rushed round to the back of the house. Osman jumped into the container and pulled his daughter out. She was soaked: her hair and face and arms and legs were streaked with the oily liquid. Her white party dress was ruined. She was, in a word, a mess.

'What on earth were you thinking of, child?'

How could Zeynep explain to them why she had walked along the slippery wall? Today of all days, when she wanted everyone to admire her white dress? They wouldn't understand that she had skipped along the wall *because* she was wearing her new dress. She didn't really understand it herself. But, then, people often do silly things without really knowing why they do them.

It Will Do You Good

Philip groaned. His mother ignored him. He groaned again, louder.

'Eat up, Philip.'

Philip sighed: *'Aaahhhh!'*

5 'Come on, you'll be late for school!'

Philip laid his head on the table and remained still as if he had just died.

'Are you all right, Philip?'

This time, a small groan was enough.

10 'What's wrong?'

He raised himself and sighed again: 'I'll be all right, Mum. I don't want to be any trouble to you.'

'Oh dear, you'd better take the day off school if you're not well.'

15 'But, Mum, I can't do that. I must go to schooo ... oo ... oh ooooohh.' The word turned into another groan, more impressive than all the others. Clutching his stomach, he even convinced himself that he was in pain. What a pity it should happen today of all days, Examination Day ...

20 'Off you go to bed, Philip. You shouldn't eat anything today.'

He spent the morning in bed. Normally, Philip didn't like being in bed. But it is nice to lie in bed doing nothing when you know that everyone else is working. In the afternoon, at about the

25 time when his schoolfriends were finishing their examination, Philip got up and went into the kitchen.

'I'm hungry, Mum.'

'It's not food you need, Philip, it's a dose of Sulman's.'

'But, Mum, my stomach feels much better.'

30 Sulman's is a liquid medicine which looks like coal tar and

tastes worse. He hated Sulman's, but there was no escape. 'I'll go into the front room and take it while I'm reading.'

She gave him the bottle and a large spoon. 'Remember, a whole spoonful. It will do you good.'

He went into the front room and put the bottle on the table. Why did medicines always taste so awful? On the other hand, why is it that everything you like is bad for you? Sulman's doesn't *cure* a bad stomach, he thought bitterly, it *gives* you one. Still, a whole spoonful of the stuff had to disappear from the bottle or he'd be in trouble with his mother. He opened the bottle, poured out a spoonful, and then, crouching down, prepared to pour the liquid through a crack in the floorboards.

It was then that he noticed the cat. The cat was very interested in what Philip was doing. Philip looked at the cat, then at the spoon, then at the cat again.

'You wouldn't like Sulman's, pussy,' he said. The cat purred.

'It's not for cats,' he explained. The cat rubbed against Philip's legs.

'Well, if you *really* want it . . .' The cat miaowed softly. Their eyes met. 'Oh well, perhaps it will do you good.'

The cat sniffed at the liquid and then began to lap it up with her little pink tongue. When she had finished, she went very quiet. Then she stood up, stretched her legs as far as they would go, threw back her head and let out a mighty miaow that was heard in the next village. Her fur stood on end. She spun round several times, ran round the room, and, just as Mother opened the door, shot between her legs and out into the garden, not to be seen again until evening.

'What on earth is wrong with that cat, Philip?'

'I don't know, Mum,' Philip said. 'I think cats do that when they're happy.'

That evening, Philip said he was feeling better. His mother gave him some yoghurt. 'Good for the stomach,' she explained.

Something rubbed against his leg. The cat had returned. Philip shrugged.

'You wouldn't like yoghurt, pussy,' he said. The cat purred . . .'

33

A Perfectly Natural Explanation

The picture moved on the wall for no apparent reason. The picture, a framed photograph of my maternal grandmother sitting in her rocking chair, made a rattling noise as it moved. Everyone at the table looked round to see what had made the noise. My sister Betty, who was facing the picture, had seen the movement.

'What on earth made it move like that?' Betty asked.

We all looked at Grandmother Pye's picture and offered explanations.

'Wind,' said Father.

It was a calm day. There was not a breath of wind, and anyway all the doors and windows were closed.

'An earthquake,' I suggested, proud that at the age of seven I knew such a long word.

'An earthquake? In *Britain*?' said my sister Betty. 'Don't be silly.'

'But', I replied defensively, 'earthquakes *do* happen sometimes, even in Britain. Don't they, Daddy?'

'We would have felt it,' my father said.

'Do you suppose Grandma Pye is all right?' Betty asked anxiously. Grandma Pye was a tough old bird, fitter than most people half her age. Of course she was all right, but Betty persisted. 'Perhaps it's a sign . . .'

'A sign of what?' I asked, looking for a chance to get my own back. 'A sign that you're stupid?'

'Stop it, you two!' mother said wearily. 'I'm sure there is a perfectly natural explanation. Now, finish your meal. Come on, eat up your vegetables, you two, or there will be no pudding for you.'

Why do parents make idle threats like that? I suppose it is just a habit.

The picture moved again, this time so violently that we all saw it. When it stopped, it was no longer straight. Grandma Pye looked as if she was about to slip off her chair. This time, nobody spoke. It wasn't funny any more. I felt really scared, but of course did not show it. My sister Betty had gone pale. My father was looking down at his plate and poking at his potatoes with his fork as if he were seeing them for the first time. Mother got up and went over to the picture. She straightened it and came back to the table. 'There', she said, 'now, let's get on with our meal.'

'But, Mummy, why did Grandma's picture move like that?'

'Oh, I expect, well, as I said, there'll be a perfectly natural explanation.'

We were sent to bed early that evening. Why do parents always make you go to bed early when something interesting is going on? It is another of those habits that make parents such a mystery to their children. Betty and I crept downstairs and sat on the bottom step trying to catch what our parents were talking about. It is so annoying when you only hear bits: '. . . *silly idea . . . frightened us all out of our wits . . . apologise . . .*', '*. . . just a joke . . . don't make such a fuss . . .*', '*. . . get over it . . .*', '*. . . explain to them in the morning . . .*'

I was up early next morning, and found the piece of thread still hanging from Grandma's picture where my father had tied it. So, Dad had moved the picture! What a good trick. It had certainly fooled everyone. Good old Dad! As we sat having breakfast, I looked at him and winked to let him know I was in on the joke. He winked back at me, but said nothing.

My mother was in the kitchen when the phone rang. She answered it, and then came into the room where we were having breakfast. She was as white as a sheet.

'That was Cousin Lucy,' she said. 'Grandma Pye died peacefully during the night.'

The Purple Bamboo Park

My name is Yunhua. I am one of the few Chinese women writers whose books have been published outside China. I live in Beijing, close to the Purple Bamboo Park. If I never marry, in a way it will be because of the Park. Let me explain.

5   If you want to be a successful writer, you have to have a proper routine. I learned early on how important it was to have regular habits: getting up early, spending so many hours writing each day, and taking regular breaks. My breaks were always the same: a walk in the Purple Bamboo Park, mostly in the evening,
10 when it is cool and when there are fewer people about. The Park is a strange place. The name comes from the bamboo which grows everywhere. It really is purple. A bamboo woodland is like no other. The tall bare stems grow close together. Looking through them is like looking through a curtain, where everything
15 is only half-seen. People who practise *tai chi* stand amongst the bamboos and you catch glimpses of their slow movements deep inside the bamboo. They are like ghosts.

   Do you know the opera *Madame Butterfly*, in which a young Japanese woman and an American naval officer meet and fall
20 in love? I am Chinese, but it was like that for Charles and me. He was Naval Attaché at one of the embassies, and we met at a reception there. I had been invited by the Ambassador's wife, who wanted to meet her 'favourite Chinese author'. Anyway, Charles and I got on like a house on fire. We met again several
25 times. The last time was in the Purple Bamboo Park, where we went for a walk one evening after dinner. He had only recently arrived in Beijing and didn't know the park.

   'Who are those people in the bamboos?'

   'They are practising *tai chi*.'

30   'Why do they go into the bamboos to do that?'

'They like to be close to nature.'

He shivered. 'They don't seem human, somehow. I'm sorry, but I don't really like this place.'

As we rounded a corner, we came face to face with three young men dressed western-style in jeans and leather jackets. 35

'Have you got a light, sir,' the tallest of them said to Charles in English.

Charles lit the young man's cigarette.

'Now, give us your wallet!' His tone was threatening. The other two looked on unsmiling. One took out a knife. Charles 40 handed over his wallet.

'Here, take it, but please don't hurt us!' he begged. I could see that Charles was really frightened.

The tall one then addressed me in Chinese. 'What have you got to offer, woman?' 45

'Nothing for you! So just clear off!' I said.

'For God's sake, Yunhua, give him whatever he wants!'

The other two came forward, standing to each side of us. Charles was trembling. 'Oh my God!' he cried.

Then, without warning, they tried to grab me. I laid out the 50 tall one with a single karate chop, spun round and gave the one with the knife a kick to the head. The third one fled, followed by the others. Charles looked at me open-mouthed.

'Where did you learn to do that?' he asked.

I didn't bother to answer his question. In fact we didn't speak 55 after that. He walked me back to my apartment building and left without a word. I never saw him again. I still take my regular walks in the Purple Bamboo Park, but, as I said before, I doubt if I shall ever marry now.

First Impressions

'Someone to see you, Mr Hedley.'

'Who is he? What does he want?'

'He says he will explain that when he sees you.'

'Tell him to make an appointment.'

5 'He says it is very urgent, Mr Hedley.'

'Oh very well, send him in.'

The stranger was a thickset man. He might have been a rugby player. His first words startled Hedley. 'The first thing I notice about a person, sir, is their shoes,' he said.

10 'What?'

'You can tell a lot about a person by their shoes,' the stranger said. 'Put it this way. They say that first impressions are the most important. What do *you* notice when you first meet someone, sir?'

15 'Look, I'm a busy man. What is it you want, exactly?'

'I notice shoes. What do you notice, sir?'

Perhaps he was a madman. Hedley thought it better to answer his question.

'Oh, I don't know. Their looks. Their clothes. The way they
20 speak. I've never really thought about it.'

'Looks? Do you mean ugly people are bad people?'

'Well, no. I just meant . . .'

'As to the way people dress, sir. Well, fashions change so quickly. And you never know whether you are looking at a
25 fashion-house original or a cheap factory-produced copy.'

Hedley looked at the stranger's suit. Dark blue, smart, ordinary.

'OK, I agree, but one thing people can't change is the way they speak,' Hedley said.

'So, someone comes to you for a job. They have a strong
30 regional accent. So what?'

'I'm talking about speaking correctly. You know, grammar, etc. I can't stand people who say things like 'If I'd have known . . .' or 'Between you and I . . .'

'Then you obviously can't stand a lot of your fellow citizens!'

'But, *you* are saying that the best way to judge someone is by looking at their shoes,' Hedley said. 'That sounds even crazier.' 35

Despite himself, Hedley was curious to hear what the man had to say. Hedley wondered about his own shoes. What did they tell the man? Where they in good taste? What about their 40
condition? Hedley polished his shoes every morning, but there might be a speck of dirt on them. He hoped the man wouldn't look at them, but he did.

'Your shoes, for instance, sir,' the man said. 'About five years' old, I'd say. Leather. Excellent quality. They have laces, they're 45
not slip-ons. And you keep them in good condition.'

'So, what does that tell you?' Hedley asked.

The stranger was beginning to irritate Hedley.

'I think you're a man who likes the best, sir,' the stranger replied. 'You're a man who looks after his things. You're not 50
lazy. You're a busy man . . .' He paused then added: '. . . and a very careful one.'

'Perhaps,' Hedley said, feeling uncomfortable now. 'Now, let me see what I can tell about you from your shoes.'

He got up to look. The man was wearing heavy black boots, 55
polished so hard you could see your face in them. They looked like the sort soldiers wear. Or policemen . . .

Hedley sighed. 'Ah, officer, I was expecting a visit from your people sooner or later. I suppose, as you people say, *"The game's up"*.' 60

'I'm afraid so, sir. You'll have to come with me to the police station to answer some questions about the disappearance of large sums of money from this company's bank account.'

Obviously, for a careful man, Hedley had not been careful enough, shoes or no shoes. 65

Seeing Is Believing

'. . . one day, Jones, chimpanzees will speak and write and reason, just like human beings.'

'And one day, pigs will fly, Smith.'

Professor Smith grunted. 'Laugh if you like, Jones, but I'm convinced that apes will soon catch up with *Homo sapiens*.'

To listen to these two professors, Smith the zoologist and Jones the philosopher, you would never guess they were friends. They argued about everything. Smith was a scientist, concerned with 'facts'. He believed in things he could see or hear or smell or taste or touch. Jones was a thinker, concerned with 'ideas'. He was suspicious of 'facts'. Seeing, for him, was not necessarily believing. He believed in things he could think about logically.

One day, they found themselves at Coney Island. Professor Smith had a young niece who, for her birthday, had begged her uncle to take her there. Not wishing to undertake such a difficult mission on his own, Smith asked his friend Jones to come along. That is how the three of them came to be staring at a notice about a remarkable dog.

> THE MOST AMAZING DOG IN THE WORLD
> IT CAN SING AND DANCE
> IT CAN TALK AND DO ARITHMETIC
> !!!! SEEING IS BELIEVING !!!

'Smith, it looks as if the dog has got there before the chimpanzee.'

'Nonsense, Jones. The whole thing will be a fake, like everything in this place.'

'Let's go inside, uncle. Please!'

Science and Philosophy bowed to the wishes of an eight-year old. They paid their money and went into the tent.

40

What they saw amazed them. The dog danced on its hind legs, keeping time to the music. When asked to add two and three, it barked five times. When the man played a tune on the piano, the dog sang in time to the music. It could even talk, after a fashion. When asked how many states there were in the Union, it made a noise which sounded remarkably like forty-eight.

The old scientist was amazed by the dog's performance, not so much by the dancing, etc, as by the dog's great intelligence. He wanted to buy the dog. The dog's owner drove a hard bargain. After all, the dog was his livelihood. But Professor Smith refused to take no for an answer, and, after an hour of bargaining, the dog was his. He didn't like dogs, but he felt happy as the carriage took them back home.

'Is it for me, uncle?'

'Not exactly, my dear,' Professor Smith answered. 'I need it for an important scientific experiment.'

'Come on, Smith,' said the philosopher. You always say *'Seeing is believing'*. The dog is a genius. What more do you need to know.'

Ignoring his friend's ironic tone, Professor Smith said: 'We may be close to the greatest scientific discovery of all time. If I can find out why this animal is so intelligent . . .'

'How do you propose to do that, my friend?'

But Professor Smith was not willing to say anything more.

A few days later, Jones went to visit his friend.

'You *what* ?' he cried, unbelieving.

'I did what any scientist would do,' said Smith. 'I put the dog to sleep and cut out its brain to find out what was special about it.'

'And?' Jones asked.

'Do you know, I couldn't find anything which would explain its extraordinary abilities,' Professor Smith replied.

At that moment, the professor's niece came into the room.

'Can I play with my doggie, uncle? Please! He's so clever.'

Neither Science nor Philosophy had an answer for the little girl.

A Better Mousetrap

The design of the mousetrap has not changed in centuries. Every inventor wants to design a better one. This is the story of one such inventor, a man called Herbert Mandini. Mandini had already invented many useful things: an automatic teaspoon,
5 a hearing aid for deaf fish, and so on. But, none of his inventions made him rich or famous. That is why, one morning, he thought about mousetraps. Actually he thought about mousetraps because he had just taken the end off one of his fingers in a mousetrap which he was using to catch flies. 'There must be a
10 better design than this', he thought to himself as he wrapped a bandage round his bleeding finger.

Three weeks and several injuries later, Mandini found himself in the waiting room of the Patent Office with a cardboard box on his lap. When it was his turn to go in, he greeted the Patent
15 Officer and put the box on the desk.

'I present "The Mandini Mousetrap"!' Mandini said proudly.

'Show me.'

Mandini took out the model of his new mousetrap and waited.

'Yes, I see,' said the Patent Officer. 'Well, erm, actually, I
20 *don't* see. Explain to me how it works.'

'Very well, sir. It's quite simple. The mouse goes through this hole in the side of the box . . .'

'The hole with the word DOOR written over the top?' the Patent Officer asked.

25 'Exactly, sir.'

The Patent Officer suddenly felt very tired. 'Do go on, Mr, er, Mandini,' he said.

'So, the mouse goes through the door and up these stairs to the balcony.'

30 The Patent Officer remained silent. Mandini looked at him

42

and then went on: 'So, the mouse is on the balcony, it looks over the balustrade and down on to the floor on the other side. And what does it see?'

'I don't know,' said the Patent Officer.

'A piece of cheese on the floor below!' said Mandini trium- 35
phantly.

'Hm. But the mouse is still alive, is it not?'

'Ah, but this is the clever bit. If you notice, set into the top of the balustrade is . . . a razorblade! The mouse rests its neck on the razorblade, and, hey presto! Throat is cut. Mouse is dead.' 40

The Patent Officer took out his handkerchief and wiped his forehead. He was getting too old for this job. 'Mr Mandini, I can see three things wrong with your mousetrap: one, it still depends on having a piece of cheese in it; two, I doubt if the blade will cut the mouse's neck; and three, even if it does, people 45
might find it a rather cruel trap. Good day, Mr Mandini.'

Three weeks later, Mandini was back at the Patent Office.

'Ah, Mr Mandini. Not another mousetrap, I hope?'

'Indeed yes! I present the Mandini Mousetrap Mark II.'

It looked exactly like the Mandini Mousetrap Mark I. 50

'Show me,' the Patent Officer said.

'The mouse goes in through the hole marked DOOR and up the stairs to the balcony,' Mandini said.

'Let me guess,' said the Patent Officer wearily. 'The mouse then looks over the balustrade on to the floor below.' 55

'Right!' Mandini smiled at him. 'But here is the difference. Instead of a razorblade, I have fitted a hacksaw blade.'

'I don't quite see how . . .'

'This is the really brilliant part, sir. *There is no cheese on the floor below.*' Mandini waited for the Patent Officer to express 60
amazement at this stroke of genius.

'Mr Mandini, I still don't quite see how . . .'

'It's obvious, sir! The mouse rests its neck on the hacksaw blade, looks down, and then quickly moves its head left-to-right left-to-right, saying: *"Where's the cheese? Where's the cheese?"'* 65

The world is still waiting for a better mousetrap.

Glossaries and Language Practice

Best Friends

GLOSSARY

Chicken! (line 5): youthful slang. Someone is 'chicken' if they are afraid to do something.

screech (line 9): the squealing noise that car brakes make when a car stops suddenly.

they questioned him (line 12): they asked him a lot of questions in order to find out what really happened.

he needn't have worried (lines 16–17): there was no reason for him to worry.

the rush hour (line 26): the time, morning and evening, when everyone is travelling to or from work.

Beware of . . . (lines 31–2): used in notices to warn people of a danger, for example 'Beware of the dog'.

pickpocket (line 32): someone who steals things from people's pockets.

He worked his way over (line 33): the platform was crowded so it was not easy to get to where the tall man was standing.

bumping into (line 34): knocked against. It also means 'to meet by chance': 'I bumped into an old friend the other day'.

slipped away (line 34): left, hoping that nobody would see him leaving.

grabbed (line 36): got hold of him quickly before he could get away.

dragged him (line 36): the pickpocket didn't want to go so he had to be dragged – pulled along.

check (line 39): have a look to make sure of something.

his childhood friend (line 49): a friend he had when he was a child.

rob (line 53): you *rob* a person, a bank, etc. You *steal* (something) *from* a person, a bank, etc.

to press charges (line 54): to make a formal complaint against someone who has committed a crime.

teach these thieves a lesson (lines 56–7): make them realise that they have done wrong.

shrugged his shoulders (line 58): moved his shoulders up quickly to show that he didn't care.

boarded his train (line 61): got into the train; also, 'board a ship', 'board a plane'.

LANGUAGE PRACTICE

A

Look at the story and find answers to these questions.

 1 Why was Deggy able to open the window?
 2 How did the boys know a car was coming?
 3 Why did Deggy get caught?
 4 What did the police want Deggy to tell them?
 5 What was Deggy's punishment for breaking into the house?
 6 Why didn't Deggy go home after he came out of prison?
 7 What did Deggy find out when he went to Ginger's house?
 8 Who were the people waiting on the station platform?
 9 What did the businessman and the pickpocket look like?
10 How did the businessman know that the wallet was his?

Work out answers to these questions.

 1 How did the boys know that the owners had gone away?
 2 Why does one of the boys say 'It's not like stealing apples' (line 4)?
 3 Ginger 'sat at home, terrified' (line 15) why?
 4 Ginger didn't visit his friend in prison. What was the reason, do you think?
 5 In which part of town did the businessman live? How do you know?
 6 In your opinion, why did the pickpocket not want to look at the businessman's face?
 7 Why did the businessman think it was a good idea to press charges?
 8 Why wasn't the pickpocket angry when the businessman decided to press charges?

B

Supply the missing words. In most cases, the first or last letter(s) of the missing word is (are) given. All the expressions are in the story.

1 When you see newspapers sticking out of the l_____, you can be sure that the o_____ have gone away.

2 Don't travel during the r_____ h_____, because the trains and buses are always crowded.

3 Joe c_____ all his pockets but couldn't find his keys anywhere.

4 Well, it was nice meeting you. Perhaps we will b_____ i_____ each other again sometime.

5 The dog doesn't chase the cat since she bit him. That certainly t_____t him a l_____!

6 My brother can't stop eating chocolate, d_____ the f_____ that it makes him sick.

7 I thought I had lost my wallet, but I _____n't h_____ worried: it was in my pocket all the time!

8 The child would have fallen in the water if her mother had not g_____ her _____ the collar.

9 I'm sorry to bother you, sir, but w_____ you be good e_____ to put out your cigarette?

10 'Who did this?' I didn't reply. I just s_____ _____ shoulders, as if to say 'It wasn't me'.

C

Fill in the missing words in this passage. In some cases, more than one word is possible.

The boys got _____ the house by _____ in through a window. When the police car pulled _____ outside the house, the two boys _____ away as fast as _____ _____. One of them was lucky: he managed to get _____, but the other fell _____, and got caught. He was sent _____ prison _____ two years. When he came _____, he went to see his friend. But, when he got _____ the house, he found _____ that the family didn't live there any _____. Years later, the two men met again. They were _____ a railway platform. They didn't recognise each _____. One of them was waiting _____ a train, but the other had become a thief and was looking _____ someone to rob. He tried to _____ the other man's wallet, but a policeman saw him and grabbed him _____ the collar.

Wordgame

A person with red hair is a *red-haired* person. A person who has blue eyes is a *blue-eyed* person. How would you describe someone:

1 who has broad shoulders
2 who has long legs
3 who always uses their left hand
4 who has fair skin
5 whose head is bald
6 who has a bad temper

Questions for Discussion

1 The businessman and the pickpocket – which is Deggy and which is Ginger? Give your reasons.
2 Whose idea was it to break into the house, do you think?
3 What do you think Ginger would have done if he had been the one to get caught? What would *you* have done in Deggy's place?

A Walk on the Beach

GLOSSARY

sailor suit (line 1): a jacket and trousers for a child in white with blue stripes, like the uniform that sailors wear.

to match (line 2): the hat was in the same style and colour as the suit.

the grown-ups (line 4): the adults; in this case, his parents and his grandmother.

grandma (line 6): a child's word for 'grandmother'. Also, 'granny' or 'nanna'.

huge (line 17): very, very big; the opposite (very, very small) is '*tiny*'.

shook his head (line 19): to show that he didn't like the idea; the opposite is 'nod your head'.

wasn't a good idea at all (lines 20–1): definitely not a good idea.

Off we go! (line 22): 'Let's go!' Compare 'Here you are!', and expressions like 'Up you get!'.

don't let go of his hand (line 23): hold his hand all the time.

make a fuss (line 26): worry too much, be too careful, tidy, etc.

managed to get away (lines 28–9): succeeded in getting away.

the water's edge (lines 29–30): the possessive *'s* is mostly used for people, animals and time expressions (a day's work, etc), and in a few set phrases like 'the water's edge'.

. . . thank goodness (lines 31–2): she was glad that the sea was calm.

swept (line 39): the way you use a brush to push things away.

felt so bad (line 49): 'bad' here means unhappy or guilty.

in all her life (lines 49–50): in her whole life.

otherwise (line 54): he was wet, but, *apart from that*, he was all right.

held him tight (line 56): You could also say 'held him tightly'.

fussy (line 58): see note to 'fuss' (line 26).

LANGUAGE PRACTICE

A

Look at the story and find answers to these questions.

1 Why had Yosef's parents bought him a new suit?
2 How did his parents feel when they saw him in his new suit?
3 Did Grandma live with Yosef and his parents?
4 What did Yosef especially enjoy about going to the beach?
5 What instruction did Yosef's mother give to Grandma before they left the house?
6 What was Grandma doing while Yosef was standing by the water?
7 What exactly happened to Yosef when the first wave crashed on the beach?
8 Was Yosef all right after the second wave had put him back on the sand?
9 What did Grandma do when she first saw that Yosef was safe?
10 What made Grandma angry?

Work out answers to these questions.

1 What was the colour of Yosef's hat, do you think?

2 Was Yosef pleased with his new suit?

3 Yosef's parents didn't want Grandma to take him to the beach. What were they afraid of?

4 When they first got to the beach, why did Grandma feel that Yosef was quite safe?

5 What words in the text tell you that the huge wave was unexpected?

6 When Grandma prayed to the different gods, what do you think she said in her prayers?

7 'Grandma tidied him up' (line 58). What do you think she did?

8 Why did she look up into the sky when she noticed that Yosef's hat was missing?

B

Supply the missing words. In most cases, the first or last letter(s) of the missing word is (are) given. All the expressions are in the story.

1 The sailor suit had a hat to m_____ .

2 Yosef's parents f_____ very pr_____ when they saw how smart he looked in his new suit.

3 'Look after Yosef, and don't l_____ g_____ of his hand!'

4 'I don't like yoghurt a_____ a_____ .'

5 Father sh_____ _____ head to show that he didn't agree.

6 _____k g_____ the second wave brought Yosef back!

7 She prayed to all the gods she could th_____ _____ .

8 She was so happy to see him again that she p_____ him up and held him t_____ .

9 Grandma th_____ the gods for br_____ him back to her.

10 Grandmothers always m_____ a f_____ of their grand-children.

C

Fill in the missing words in this passage. In some cases, more than one word is possible.

Yosef's parents bought him a sailor suit _____ his birthday. Grandma had come to stay with them _____ a week or _____ . 'It's a lovely day,' she said. 'Why don't we go _____ a walk?' Father didn't like the idea _____ _____ . Grandma wasn't young _____ more: she was _____ old, and was not _____ _____ trusted. Anyway, they went _____ the beach. Yosef _____ to get away _____ his grandma. He stood _____ the water's _____, and a huge wave _____ him _____ to sea. When another wave _____ him back, she noticed that his hat was missing, so she shouted _____ loudly _____ she _____ : 'where's his hat?'

Wordgame

A careless *person is one who does not show care. What would you call:*

1 someone who is not wearing a hat
2 someone who has no sense of humour
3 something which you cannot use
4 a day when there isn't any wind
5 a situation where there is no hope
6 a couple who have no children

Questions for Discussion

1 What kind of birthday presents would Yosef have preferred, do you think?
2 What do you think Grandma said to Yosef's parents when she got back home?
3 Why do you think Yosef liked his Grandma so much? Do you have any grandparents? Are they like Yosef's grandmother?

Family Fortune

GLOSSARY

times were hard (line 1): life was difficult.

come along (line 4): arrived.

sounded like (line 5): seemed to be.

land of milk and honey (line 5): the wonderful land which God promised to give to the Jews.

emigrated (line 8): went to settle there; an *immigrant* (line 29) is someone who has emigrated.

drifting (line 8): here, it means going from place to place without any particular purpose.

another soul (line 10): here it means 'another human being'.

his savings (line 11): all the money he had saved up.

due to (line 14): to be paid to.

relative (line 15): someone who was related to Bentley Harcourt.

took up a new hobby (line 19): started to trace his family tree for fun.

tracing his family tree (line 19): finding out about members of his family (grandparents, etc).

fortune (line 27): here it means 'a very big amount of money'.

be entitled to (line 32): have a legal right to.

mounting (line 33): increasing, getting bigger and bigger all the time.

As it turned out . . . (line 37): He finally found out the true situation, which was that . . .

he talked the matter over with his wife (lines 35–6): he discussed the matter with his wife.

funnily enough (line 41): it may be hard to believe but . . .

fish canning (line 48): a cannery is a place where fish such as sardines are put into cans (tins).

they became the best of friends (lines 51–2): they became very good friends.

LANGUAGE PRACTICE

A

Look at the story and find answers to these questions.

1 What did Bentley Harcourt do for a living?
2 Why did Bentley Harcourt decide to wait before getting married?
3 Where did Bentley Harcourt find out about the American West?
4 How did Bentley Harcourt get to America?
5 Did Bentley Harcourt go straight to Texas when he arrived in America?
6 How did he pay for the land in Texas?
7 What was David Kingsley's new hobby?
8 Was David Kingsley the only one who claimed the Harcourt fortune?

9 What were the 'arguments, the quarrels and the court cases' (lines 39–40) about?

10 What was the treasure that David Kingsley found?

Work out answers to these questions.

1 What made Bentley Harcourt decide to emigrate?
2 Where did he get the money to pay for his passage to America?
3 What made him decide to settle in Texas?
4 Where did the $2bn (line 41) come from?
5 How did David Kingsley find out that he had a relative called Bentley Harcourt?
6 Why did David Kingsley write to the magazine?
7 Why didn't David Kingsley mind that he hadn't inherited the Harcourt fortune?
8 What do we know about David Kingsley's great-great-uncle Harcourt?

B

Supply the missing words. In most cases, the first or last letter(s) of the missing word is (are) given. All the expressions are in the story.

1 I'd like to e_____ to Australia, s_____e in New South Wales, buy an opal mine and m_____ a lot of money!
2 But I wouldn't leave my money in my bank a_____: I would use my s_____s to buy a ranch.
3 Poor Bentley Harcourt died sh_____ after b_____g his ranch in Texas.
4 A lot of people cl_____d to be r_____s of Bentley Harcourt.
5 I like having a bit of money, but, f_____ e_____, I wouldn't like to be rich.
6 The Kingsleys and the Harcourts became the b_____ _____ friends.
7 A large a_____t of money is missing. We must ch_____ all the records for the last year.
8 What happened to the profits which were d_____ _____ the owner of the land?

C

Replace the words underlined with an expression from the text based on the word(s) given in brackets. Make any necessary grammatical changes.

Example: Don't worry! (fuss)
        Don't make a fuss!

1 Life was not easy for farmers in those days. (times)
2 The American West sounded like a wonderful place. (milk and honey)
3 He travelled for days and didn't meet anyone else at all. (soul)
4 He decided to find out everything he could about his family. (trace)
5 David thought that he had a legal claim to the Bentley Harcourt fortune. (entitled)
6 He happened to find a reference to his great-great-uncle while checking church records. (across)
7 He discussed everything with his wife. (over)
8 David's great-great-uncle owned a fish cannery and became very rich. (fortune)

Wordgame
Someone who works hard *is a* hardworking *person. Someone who* dresses well *is a* well-dressed *person. What would you call:*
1 someone who talks fast
2 someone who thinks quickly
3 someone who dresses badly
4 someone who speaks well
5 someone who has good looks (is handsome)

Questions for Discussion
1 What do you know about your family tree? How far back can you trace your family?
2 'He talked the matter over with his wife' (lines 35–6). What do you think they said to each other?
3 How would you feel if you discovered you were entitled to the Harcourt fortune? What would you do with the money?

A Free Lunch

GLOSSARY

at your service (line 1): ready to help you in any way I can.

addressing (line 2): speaking in a formal way to the group.

Lubango (line 9): a city in the south of Angola in Africa.

stayed on (line 16): most of the Portuguese left Angola, but Cardosa continued to live there.

after Independence (line 16): Angola was a Portuguese colony until 1975, when it became independent.

uncertainly (line 23): she was not certain if there had been a misunderstanding.

he led the way (line 30): he went first to show them the way to the conference room.

having no better alternative (line 31): they didn't have another choice.

He kept up a conversation (line 31): he went on talking to them while they walked.

over his shoulder (line 32): he looked back at them as he led them to the conference room.

bowed low (lines 42–3): bent forward from the waist, lowering his head to show respect.

the . . . table which had been laid (lines 51–2) to 'lay a table' is to put out the plates, knives, etc, ready for the next meal.

A couple of weeks later (line 60): about two weeks, but it might have been a bit more or a bit less.

LANGUAGE PRACTICE

A

Look at the story and find answers to these questions.

1 What was strange about addressing the delegation as 'gentlemen'?
2 When had Cardosa learned English?
3 How do we know that Cardosa was an Angolan citizen?
4 Why was Cardosa able to understand the word 'congress'?
5 Why did Cardosa continue to wear a watch that didn't go?
6 Where was Cardosa when the delegation came out of the morning session?

7 What did they have for lunch?
8 What kind of conference had the Cubans come for?
9 What did Cardosa do while the women were in the afternoon session?
10 Why did Cardosa need to try to get free lunches?

Work out answers to these questions.

1 Cardosa said: 'Good morning, gentlemen.' (line 64). What should he have said?
2 What was wrong with Cardosa's command of English?
3 Did the North Korean delegation understand Cardosa?
4 Cardosa took the women to the conference room. What two phrases in the text tell you that he walked in front of them?
5 Why do you think Cardosa decided to use the word 'comrades' (line 43)?
6 Why was the leader 'glad when the lunch was over', do you think?
7 *Bacalhau*, cod, is a sea fish. Lubango is in the centre of the country. What, therefore, is wrong with Cardosa's statement about the fish?
8 How did Cardosa make a living (apart from his taxi job), do you think?

B

Supply the missing words. In most cases, the first or last letter(s) of the missing word is (are) given. All the expressions are in the story.

1 He was proud o_____ the English he _____d learned _____ a youngster.
2 He didn't understand w_____ people said _____ him, but this didn't b_____ him.
3 They all stared _____ the funny little man who gr_____ them when they arrived.
4 The English word 'delegation' is almost the s_____ word _____ Portuguese.
5 Cardosa l_____ the way _____ the conference room, and the women f_____ him.
6 Their English was not good enough to k_____p up a conversation _____ English.

7 When they came _____ after the morning s_____, he
w_____ waiting _____ them.

8 He sat next _____ the leader _____ the table wh_____
had been l_____ for them.

9 He spoke as _____ he had personally c_____ the fish
sp_____ for them.

10 When the women went b_____ to the conference, Cardosa _____ for a sleep in his taxi.

C

*Cardosa seemed to misunderstand several questions which the leader
asked him. Work out questions to which these would be the answers.*
Example: If someone says, 'I am fifteen', the question was 'How
old are you?'

1 'Ah yes, a beautiful country.' (line 18)

2 'I am very well.' (line 37)

3 'Eight-thirty.' (line 40)

4 'Yes, the food here is very good.' (line 49)

5 'I do, too.' (line 56)

Write full questions using the prompts in brackets and the answers given.

6 (delegation/come from/?) 'From North Korea.'

7 (conference/start/?) 'At eight-thirty.'

8 (have/lunch/?) 'We are having codfish today.'

9 (sleep/after lunch/?) 'Because he was tired.'

10 (Cubans/arrive/?) 'A couple of weeks later.'

Wordgame

If you behave in a confident way, *you behave* confidently. *In the same
way:*

1 If someone speaks in a loud voice, they are speaking _____ .

2 If it is probable that something will happen, it will _____
happen.

3 If it is rare for something to happen, it _____ happens.

4 If you think it is unfortunate that nobody speaks Portuguese in
your company, you say: '_____, nobody speaks Portuguese.'

5 If someone is happy to do something for you, they might say: 'I
will _____ do that for you.'

Questions for Discussion

1 Imagine that the North Korean leader is describing her visit later to a friend. Tell the story of her meeting with Cardosa from her point of view.

2 What kind of conversation took place between Cardosa and the Cuban delegation, do you think?

3 Do you think Cardosa really misunderstood the women's questions? Why should he *pretend* to misunderstand?

Departures

GLOSSARY

alive (line 1): still living. This adjective is not used before a noun, i.e., you can say 'the bird is alive' but *not* 'an alive bird'. The same is true of *aloud* (line 13) and *upset* (line 48).

'*The thing is . . .*' (line 4): This is a very common way of introducing an explanation.

I've no idea what . . . (line 4): I really don't know what . . .

swift (line 8): a small bird which builds its nest high up in the roofs of buildings.

I'm sorry to bother you but . . . (line 10): this is a common way of apologising for disturbing someone.

to be phoning (lines 12–13): to be in the act of phoning.

as best he could (line 21): the same as 'as well as he could'.

skinny (line 26): very thin, without flesh; so thin as to be ugly.

'*. . . if you ask me.*' (lines 29–30): the same as 'in my opinion'.

It won't eat (line 47): it refuses to eat.

upset (line 48): sad.

doesn't make it (line 48): doesn't live. 'To make it' means to be successful.

Try feeding it on fish (line 53): If you want to keep it alive, feed it on fish and see what happens.

came round (line 54): visited him.

I've had enough. (line 56): People say this when they don't want to go on with something, because they find it boring, irritating, etc.

winging its way (line 65): a rather poetic way of saying 'flying'.

LANGUAGE PRACTICE

A

Look at the story and find answers to these questions.

1 Where did Renos find the bird?
2 Where has Renos put the bird?
3 Why didn't Renos put the bird back in its nest?
4 What two kinds of food did Renos give the bird?
5 What other problems does Renos have in trying to keep the bird alive?
6 What does Maryjean think of the baby bird?
7 Why is Renos surprised when Maryjean says she is leaving?
8 What was Maryjean doing in Athens?
9 Why would a goldfinch have been easier to feed?
10 What two things did Renos notice when he looked up into the evening sky?

Work out answers to these questions.

1 How does Paul know that the bird is a swift?
2 Why didn't Renos ask someone in Athens to help him?
3 Why does Paul think that the bird will die?
4 Why should the pieces of cat meat be 'tiny'?
5 What does Maryjean mean when she says: 'A waste of time, if you ask me' (lines 29–30)?
6 What do you think made her so angry (lines 32–3)?
7 What makes people slam doors when they leave?
8 What made Maryjean decide not to stay on in Athens?

B

Supply the missing words. In most cases, the first or last letter(s) of the missing word is (are) given. All the expressions are in the story.

1 If it ate seeds l_____ a goldfinch, it would be easy to f_____ .
2 He was _____ busy that he h_____ noticed how late it was.
3 I don't know _____ else who is interested _____ birds.
4 Renos was very u_____ when the bird died; he went on to the b_____y and looked _____ into the sky.
5 She was f_____ of him, but she was not sure if she r_____ loved him.

6 I'm sorry to b_____ you, but I n_____ your help.
7 I think you are w_____ your time trying to _____p that bird alive.
8 If it w_____ eat, it is s_____ to die.

C

Replace the words underlined with an expression from the text based on the word(s) given in brackets. Make any necessary grammatical changes.

Example: Don't worry! (fuss)
　　　　　Don't make a fuss!

1 I don't know where she is. (idea)
2 I'll let you know what happens. (things)
3 He's crazy in my opinion (ask)
4 It sleeps a lot. (spends)
5 It couldn't swallow the cat meat. (difficulty)
6 Do you think the bird will live? (make)
7 You should put it back in the nest. (Why)
8 She wondered whether to stay on after the summer. (talk about)
9 I suggest you feed it on fish. (Try)
10 They eat insects and that is why they are difficult to feed. (make)

Wordgame
From to depart, *we get* departure. *Complete this table (the words are taken from the first five stories).*

depart　*departure*
1 fly　　_____
2 pray　_____
3 refer　_____
4 excite _____
5 argue　_____

Questions for Discussion
1 Paul's hobby is studying birds. What do you think he finds so interesting about birds?
2 'She suddenly felt angry again, the same anger that she had felt the other night' (lines 32–3). What is making Maryjean so angry, do you think?

3 Renos and Maryjean have different nationalities (Greek and American). If they got married, what problems could this cause? What other kinds of 'mixed marriages' can you think of?

Happy Days

[*Robin Hood* is a popular hero. He was a 13th-century outlaw. He and his followers lived in *Sherwood Forest* in the English Midlands. He always dressed in green. One of his men was *Friar Tuck*, a monk.]

GLOSSARY

Get on with it (line 3): begin. Anyone who uses this expression is usually impatient or irritated.

the rich . . . the poor (lines 4–5): rich people . . . poor people.

who was playing (line 6): his part in the play is a rich merchant.

merchant (line 6): a trader, one who trades (buys and sells) things.

It doesn't matter (line 11): it isn't important.

as if to a small child (line 22): as if he were speaking to a small child.

three days to go (line 27): three more days before the play is performed.

crossing her fingers (line 30): people cross their fingers in the hope that nothing will go wrong.

on the night (line 30): on the night when the play is performed.

shuffled (line 34): walked slowly, not lifting his feet clear of the floor.

Back in the teachers' room (line 45): when she was back in the teachers' room.

shaking (line 46): here, it means trembling. She was upset.

You are supposed to be . . . (lines 60–1): this is what everyone is expecting.

indignantly (line 62): you are indignant when you feel you have been treated badly or unfairly.

What was the point of teachers? (lines 65–6): Do we really need teachers?

LANGUAGE PRACTICE

A

Look at the story and find answers to these questions.

1 Where were the children standing when the story opens?
2 What, according to Harry's lines, does Robin Hood do?
3 Why did Christopher point at Harry's head?
4 What question did the teacher ask about David?
5 Why did Harry regard the teacher's question about David as a stupid one?
6 What two things did the Headmaster want to know about the play?
7 When will the play be performed?
8 What kind of sound did Christopher make as he shuffled across the stage?
9 What did Amanda do when she went back to the teachers' room?
10 How did Christopher explain the strange noise he was making?

Work out answers to these questions.

1 In what way is the colour of Harry's hat important?
2 What did the teacher mean when she said 'It doesn't matter'.
3 Why doesn't David need to wear a hat?
4 Why did Amanda cross her fingers when she answered the Head's question, do you think?
5 Is the teacher confident that the play will be a success? If not, why not?
6 Why do you think the Head *whispered* to the teacher?
7 Why does the Head sometimes call the teacher Mrs Pratt and sometimes Amanda?
8 Why didn't Amanda want to talk about the play with Julia, do you think?

B

Supply the missing words. In most cases, the first or last letter(s) of the missing word is (are) given. All the expressions are in the story.

1 Only another week _____ g_____ and the school holidays begin!

2 Everyone jumped when Joe m_____ a n_____ like a bomb going off.

3 Why does everyone speak to me a_____ i_____ I were an idiot?

4 I don't want to talk about it: _____'s talk about s_____ e_____ .

5 What's the p_____ _____ having a car if you don't know how to drive?

6 You're s_____ _____ be riding a horse, so why are you making a noise like a train?

7 I'm taking my driving test this morning. So, wish me luck and keep _____ fingers _____d!

8 It doesn't m_____ how old you are, it is never too late to learn a foreign language.

9 The Head asked Amanda h_____ the play was g_____!

10 I was already h_____ w_____ _____ss the field before I saw the bull.

C

The verbs in brackets are all irregular verbs which have been used in the first six stories. Use them to complete the sentences, making sure to change them into the past tense.

Example: Amanda _____ it was a mistake to ask such a question. (know)

Amanda *knew* it was a mistake to ask such a question.

1 The first performance _____ half an hour late. (begin)

2 The man only _____ his overcoat in really cold weather. (wear)

3 I _____ this watch from my grandfather. (buy)

4 Joe _____ the eight-thirty train into London every morning. (catch)

5 We looked in every room before we finally _____ what we were looking for. (find)

6 We _____ a loud noise like a railway engine going up a hill. (hear)

7 I _____ too long in the sun, and now I am as red as a beetroot. (spend)

8 When the two boys _____ again, they hardly recognised each other. (meet)

9 The others had no money, so Amanda _____ for everything. (pay)

10 David _____ a letter to the magazine about his great-great-uncle. (write)

11 Who _____ this dog into the classroom? (bring)

12 I'm sorry, I _____ to bring any money with me. (forget)

Wordgame

There are other VERB + NOUN expressions like go mad *and* stay silent. *Use a verb from [I] and a noun from [II] to complete the sentences:*

[I] get go grow look stand turn

[II] blue happy loose old sour still

1 If you don't put the milk in the refrigerator, it will _____ _____ .

2 Stop walking up and down. Can't you _____ _____ for one second?

3 I've started to _____ _____ , but I'd like to be young again.

4 Your face is so miserable! Please try to _____ _____ .

5 The lion has escaped! I have no idea how it managed to _____ _____ .

6 It was so cold that day that our faces _____ _____ .

Questions for Discussion

1 Imagine that you are Christopher. Tell a friend from another school about the play.

2 Robin Hood is a popular hero. What other popular heroes do you know about?

3 Whose side are you on in this story: the teachers' or the children's?

A Load of Old Rubbish

GLOSSARY

Victorian (line 3): built in the reign of Queen Victoria (1819–1901), nineteenth-century.

antique (line 5): something which is valuable because it is very old.

coalmining (line 10): mining – digging coal out of the ground.

make up (line 11): invent. The stories were not true, they came from our imagination.

fiancé (line 13): a man who has promised to marry a woman is her *fiancé*; she is his *fiancée*.

the Great War (line 13): the 1914–1918 war in Europe, later called the First World War.

broken-hearted (line 14): it breaks your heart to lose someone you love.

a white witch (line 16): a witch who uses her magical powers to do good things for people.

spots (line 17): ugly things on the skin; most adolescents have spots and hate them.

a friend of my mother's (line 23): one of my mother's friends; note the *'s* after *mother*.

a great gossip (line 23): she was a woman who loved to talk about other people.

I give up (line 27): I'm not going to try any more.

to empty the house (line 36): to take everything out of the house.

headline (line 46): the line in big letters at the top of a newspaper article to tell you what the article is about.

penknife (line 48): a small pocket knife, once used to cut the end of a feather to make a pen.

original (line 60): these were the ones that the artist(s) had painted; they were not copies.

learned of our discovery (line 61): heard what we had found.

LANGUAGE PRACTICE

A

Look at the story and find answers to these questions.

1 What kind of house did Miss Darby live in?
2 What could you see on all the walls inside her house?
3 What is a 'Staffordshire Darby'?
4 When did the writer find out about the Darby family?
5 Where were Miss Darby's 'six children', according to the writer?
6 Why does Mrs Triggs say 'I give up!' (line 27)?
7 Why did the nephews come across to visit the writer's house?
8 Did they intend to move into their aunt's house? Why?
9 How did the nephews make use of the two vans?
10 How did the children discover that the newspapers were very old?

Work out answers to these questions.

1 Did she come from a rich family? How do you know?
2 How do we know that Miss Darby 'loved art'?
3 Why does the writer describe his sister Alice as 'a romantic'?
4 Why do you think Alan was interested in the 'white witch'?
5 How did the writer's family know so much about Miss Darby?
6 Why did the children open one of the newspaper bundles?
7 How much were the paintings in the first bundle worth?
8 Why did Miss Darby keep the paintings inside newspapers instead of hanging them on her walls?

B

Supply the missing words. In most cases, the first or last letter(s) of the missing word is (are) given. All the expressions are in the story.

1 I'm _____ of those people never throws anything a_____ .
2 '*Waste not, want not*' is my mother's favourite s_____ .
3 This story isn't true; I m_____ it _____ .
4 Nobody was allowed inside her house, e_____ for her house-keeper.
5 They were thinking _____ m_____ into a bigger house?
6 Miss Darby refused to get r_____ of the rubbish.
7 We found o_____ that the paintings were o_____ , not copies.
8 Each _____ of them was w_____ a lot of money.

C

Rewrite the sentence starting with the word(s) given in brackets. All the expressions are in the story.

Example: I don't have a car but I know how to drive. (Although . . .)

1 She never threw anything away. (She was . . .)
2 There were paintings on all the walls. (Every inch . . .)
3 According to my father, she came from a rich family. (I remember my . . .)
4 I didn't know what he was talking about. (I had . . .)
5 She stares at your spots and cures them. (She can cure . . .)
6 Her children are locked in a dark cellar. (She keeps . . .)
7 We only found out about the nephews after she died. (It was . . .)
8 A huge furniture van took everything away. (Everything . . .)
9 'Can I have one of these newspaper bundles?' Alan asked. (Alan asked if . . .)
10 Alan used his penknife to cut the string. (Alan cut . . .)

Wordgame

There are many expressions in English like give up *(line 27) and* join in *(line 41). Use words from [I] and [II] to complete the sentences.*

[I] came got sat slipped stayed

[II] across away down on out

1 The car stopped and a policeman _____ _____ .
2 The thief _____ _____ quietly before anyone saw him.
3 She was tired of standing so she _____ _____ on the sand.
4 I _____ _____ this old photograph while I was tidying my desk.
5 She liked Greece so much that she _____ _____ for another month.

Questions for Discussion

1 Imagine the conversation between the two nephews when they found out what was in the bundles of newspapers. How would you have felt?
2 The children had different ideas about Miss Darby. Which one do you think is most likely?
3 Supposing you had £10,000 to spend on antiques. What would you buy and why?

Rent Free

GLOSSARY

'*What about you?*' (line 6): a way of returning the question, 'is this your first time in Crete?'

broke (line 9): a popular slang word meaning to be without any money at all.

to call for them (line 13): to go round to their hotel to take them to the vineyard.

We don't speak a word of Greek (lines 18–19): We don't speak any Greek at all.

Eventually (line 22): after some time.

All the best! (line 40): a way of wishing someone luck, wishing them 'the best of luck'.

make an early start (line 47): to leave the house early in order to start their journey back.

do some sightseeing (line 48): visit places of historical or artistic importance.

in the rest of the island (line 48): in the other parts of the island.

they were to eat (line 50): it was arranged that they would eat.

Mezes (line 51): appetizers before the main meal, but *mezes* can be a whole meal.

pastries (line 52): cakes and similar sweet things.

halfway through the evening (line 54): in the middle of the evening.

it's over (line 57): it is finished.

puzzled (line 58): they had said something which didn't make sense to him.

crept away (line 66): you creep away when you don't want people to see or hear you go.

LANGUAGE PRACTICE

A

Look at the story and find answers to these questions.

1 How many times had the girls been to Crete before?
2 How many times had Tov been to Crete?

3 Why does Rosemary say 'I think we have been very lucky' (line 18)?

4 How did they travel into the mountains?

5 How did Rosemary know that Tov and old Loizou were talking about work?

6 Why did Tov need to translate everything?

7 When will the girls get paid for their work?

8 How do the girls feel about grape picking after two weeks in the vineyard?

9 What was it that 'puzzled' Andreas (line 58)?

10 How did the girls get out of the barn on the day they left?

Work out answers to these questions.

1 What is there in the text that tells you they are on a boat at the beginning of the story?

2 How long the girls stay in Crete depends on . . . what?

3 Why do you think Marja refers to Tov as 'your friend' (line 16)?

4 Why don't the girls stay at old Loizou's farm?

5 Why did Loizou 'indicate with hand gestures' (lines 49–50)?

6 What do you know about Loizou's son?

7 What was it that Tov 'forgot to mention' (line 42)?

8 'They could not look at each other' (line 67). Why not?

B

Supply the missing words. In most cases, the first or last letter(s) of the missing word is (are) given. All the expressions are in the story.

1 I like modern jazz. What a_____ you?

2 We had to leave h_____ way _____gh the concert.

3 Let's go to London tomorrow to _____ some sightseeing.

4 Let's sp_____ some time sightseeing while we are here.

5 When Rosemary first arrived in Crete, she couldn't speak a w_____ _____ Greek.

6 I'm afraid th_____ isn't a_____ for you to sleep at the farm.

7 Wh_____ is that car? It belongs _____ my sister.

8 The girls got _____ before d_____, while everyone was st_____ sleeping.

C

Put the words in brackets in their usual place in the sentence.
Example: Have you been to Crete? (ever)
Have you *ever* been to Crete?

1 Have you been to the USA? (before)
2 I've been several times. (there)
3 In Crete, you will see vineyards. (everywhere)
4 Loizou and his wife could speak Greek. (only)
5 You can stay for another week. (here)
6 I forgot to tell you about the rent. (nearly)
7 He indicated that the meal was ready. (with a gesture)
8 Haven't you finished your work? (yet)
9 Andreas had got back from Athens. (just)
10 I want to make an early start. (tomorrow)

Wordgame
The words lucky *(line 18) and* luck *are related. Complete this table.*

Example:	excited	*excitement*
1	_____	value
2	difficult	_____
3	angry	_____
4	_____	fortune
5	_____	sun

Questions for Discussion
1 What part did Tov play in the story? What kind of young man was he, do you think?
2 If you were old Loizou – or his brother – what would you think about the girls' sudden departure?
3 What do you think about the girls' action in leaving without paying their 'rent'? What would you have done in their place?

The Perfect Woman

GLOSSARY

get together (line 1): meet.
used to sit (line 4): it was their habit or custom to sit.
believe it or not (line 6): you might find this hard to believe, but . . .

set off (lines 8–9): started a journey.

in search of (line 9): to look for.

make do with (line 12): be satisfied with, accept.

second best (line 12): good enough, but still less than the best.

I must have visited (line 14): I haven't added them up, but I am sure I visited . . .

self-confident (line 18): sure of themselves.

made small talk (line 31): talked about unimportant things.

I planned my campaign (line 33): like an army general planning the next stage of a war.

win her heart (line 33): make her love me.

finishing touch (line 40): the final thing you do to make everything perfect.

the conversation flowed easily (lines 45–6): the way water runs down a mountainside.

left me well off (line 48): left him enough money to live comfortably.

come into (line 50): inherited.

LANGUAGE PRACTICE

A

Look at the story and find answers to these questions.

1 Why didn't the writer want to tell anyone about his secret dream?
2 How did the writer come to be rich?
3 How much of America did he visit?
4 What was wrong with American women, according to the writer?
5 In what way did Australian women frighten him?
6 What did he think of Thai women?
7 How did he come to meet the woman he was looking for?
8 What was the 'finishing touch' to his meal preparations?
9 What did the woman think of his cooking?
10 When did he decide to tell her about his search?

Work out answers to these questions.

1 What are the 'impossible dreams' that men talk about?
2 What had prevented the writer from getting married?
3 Why does he say 'funnily enough' (line 25)?

4 'I just made small talk' (line 31). Why did he do that?
5 What sorts of things did he do to win her heart, do you think?
6 What did he do to make a good impression when she came to dinner?
7 How could the woman afford to go round the world, too?
8 Why was it so difficult for him to smile (line 53)?

B

Add a word from [I] to a word from [II] to make two-word phrases that will fit in the sentences. We have done the first one to help you. All the expressions are in the story.

[I] another believe ~~funnily~~ get make must my second set small well

[II] ~~enough~~ best do have it off off own soul talk together

1 I had never seen her before, but, *funnily enough*, she smiled at me as if she knew me.
2 I'm afraid we haven't got any butter; you will have to _____ _____ with margarine.
3 He's only eighteen, but, _____ _____ or not, he is already a millionaire.
4 I don't like parties where you have to make _____ _____ with people you don't know.
5 He doesn't know what it is to be poor; his family are very _____ _____ .
6 We expected you hours ago? Did you _____ _____ late?
7 I got to Joe's office at six, but he had already left. I _____ _____ missed him by minutes.
8 Your report isn't good enough for the boss. She won't accept _____ _____ from anyone.
9 I'm sorry I have to leave so soon. Why don't we _____ _____ for a drink sometime?
10 I enjoyed travelling abroad, but I still like _____ _____ country best.

C

There are two mistakes in each of these sentences to be corrected. All the expressions are in the story.

Example: You know how *is it* when men *getting* together.

You know how *it is* when men *get* together.

1 I was just like the others men who use to sit around talking rubbish.

2 I had always wanted to get marry, but I could never found the right woman.

3 I visited a lot of countries without to find what I was looking for it.

4 I didn't like Australian woman; they let me feel really uncomfortable.

5 When I saw that she was dropping her purse, I ran for pick it up.

6 If you lie the table properly, whose going to notice the food?

7 He needed any money, so he decided to sell some of his aunt paintings.

8 As we sat drinking coffee after the meal, I told to her from my search.

Wordgame

There are many words in English made up of two words, like tablecloth, *a cloth to put on a table. Make up words from [I] and [II].*

[I] candle   car   head   house   letter   pen   table

[II] box   cloth   keeper   knife   line   park   stick

Questions for Discussion

1 What is your opinion of the writer? Why couldn't he find the woman of his dreams?

2 'If I won the lottery, I'd . . .' What would you do if you came into a fortune?

3 What is your idea of the perfect partner? What do you think he or she would look for in you?

Cabbage White

GLOSSARY

change into caterpillars (line 9): become caterpillars.

Well done! (line 12): An expression used to praise someone who has done something well.

every single cabbage (lines 12–13): 'single' is used to make it clear that he meant *all* the cabbages.

Let's see how you get on (line 17): I want to see what progress you make, how successful you are.

first (line 17): before I can decide how much to pay you.

armed with (line 19): comparing their job to going into battle with weapons, for example, guns, swords, etc.

At least! (line 22): there must be at least a million cabbages, if not more.

knew better than to argue (line 25): realised that it was useless to argue.

It was a horrible business (lines 26–7): 'business' here refers to the job they had to do.

wriggled (line 27): moved their bodies rapidly to try to get away.

It took the two children ages (lines 27–8): it took them a very long time.

we don't care if you (line 32): it won't bother us if . . ., it doesn't matter to us if . . .

She missed (line 34): She didn't succeed in hitting them.

coming up with (line 36): thinking of, finding an answer to a problem.

she reasoned (line 41): thought the matter through in a logical way.

just in case (line 43): because it was possible that.

left (line 56): remaining; and *was left* (line 59): remained.

tiptoed (line 61): walked away on tiptoe – on the tips of their toes – so that he would not hear them leave.

LANGUAGE PRACTICE

A

Look at the story and find answers to these questions.

1 Who is older, Sarah or Jamie?
2 Why aren't the children at school?
3 What exactly was the job the gardener gave them to do?
4 How did Sarah work out how many caterpillars there were in the garden?
5 What was Sarah's 'brilliant' idea?
6 What did the gardener use the bamboo poles for?

7 When was it easiest to hit the butterflies? When was it most difficult?

8 How did the children feel when they had finished their work?

9 Why did the cabbage patch 'look like a battlefield' (lines 58–9)?

10 What did the children mean when they said 'Thank goodness' (line 64)?

Work out answers to these questions.

1 What do you know about the gardener's age and appearance?

2 When will the gardener decide how much to pay them?

3 Was Sarah's arithmetic correct?

4 Why do you think they found the job 'a horrible business' (lines 26–7)?

5 Why does it say 'of course' in line 34?

6 What does 'This' refer to in line 51?

7 Did Jamie think that Sarah's idea was a good one?

8 Why did they 'tiptoe' out of the garden (line 61)?

B

Supply the missing words. In most cases, the first or last letter(s) of the missing word is (are) given. All the expressions are in the story.

1 I have a hen that l_____ six eggs every day.

2 Someone has c_____ up _____ an idea for making sausages from old newspapers.

3 Joe wanted to e_____ some extra money to pay _____ his holiday.

4 We are _____ holiday next week, th_____ goodness!

5 I know b_____ than to argue _____ my boss.

6 You sh_____ take an umbrella _____ case it rains.

7 They stayed out u_____ it was dark.

8 How do you manage to work here without g_____ mad?

C

Replace the words underlined with an expression from the text based on the word(s) given in brackets. Make any necessary grammatical changes.

Example: Don't underline{worry}! (fuss)
        Don't make a fuss!

1 Thank goodness I have finished my homework. (glad)
2 It isn't kind to laugh at people when they do stupid things. (fun)
3 I've read all the books in this library. (single)
4 We needed a lot of time to finish the job. (ages)
5 After a while, the caterpillars will become butterflies. (change)
6 Most of the cabbages had gone . (hardly/left)
7 Are you making progress ? (get on)
8 We must remove all the butterflies. (rid)
9 Please begin as soon as you ready. (started)
10 It doesn't bother me if you say bad things about me. (care)

Wordgame
In each sentence, there are two words which have a letter missing. For example, the sentence 'Sarah sung her pole round and round tying to hit the butterflies' *should be* 'Sarah swung her pole round and round trying to hit the butterflies.' *Find and correct the words that have a letter missing. All the words are used in the story.*
1 'What kid of work are you to children looking for?' he asked.
2 My bother and I are on holiday and we want to ear some money.
3 The man who owned the garden had no air: he was completely bad.
4 The children stated on the first row of cabbages and their buckets were son filled with caterpillars.
5 Sarah stuck out at a butterfly but she missed, of curse.
6 The round was covered with dad butterflies.

Questions for Discussion
1 If you were the gardener, what would you say to the children if you met them again?
2 Have you ever done a holiday job? What other ideas do you have for earning money?
3 Even animal lovers will kill species they don't like, such as flies and mosquitoes. How do you decide when it is all right to kill another living creature?

The Pony and the Donkey

GLOSSARY

pony (title): a small horse, very popular with children.

were mad about horses (line 1): liked horses very very much; they thought about them all the time.

in disbelief (line 6): they couldn't believe it.

ponytrekking (line 8): riding on a pony through the countryside with other people.

Same here (line 12): The same is true for me, I am also bad at English.

I tell you what (line 18): People use this expression to introduce a proposal, an idea, a suggestion.

Emma came to her rescue (lines 19–20): If someone is in difficulties, you rescue them, i.e., try to save them.

cleared her throat (line 34): made sure her voice was all right before she started to speak.

brand new (line 35): completely new.

trotting (line 35): trotting is faster than walking but slower than running.

it was her turn (lines 37–8): Rochelle had finished reading, now Emma was to read.

Yours is bound to win (line 42): Your poem is certain to win.

I bet you win (line 43): I am sure that you will win.

treat (line 55): something special which gives you pleasure.

she leafed through the pages (line 57): she turned over the pages looking for her poem.

How could she face Emma? (lines 63–4): look her in the eye without being embarrassed or ashamed.

'*Fancy preferring . . .*' (line 67): I can hardly believe that they preferred . . .

LANGUAGE PRACTICE

A

Look at the story and find answers to these questions.

1 What was the girls' secret dream?

2 How often did the Children's Poetry Competition happen?
3 Why was Emma so doubtful about entering the competition?
4 Why didn't Rochelle want to write about a donkey?
5 How did they get the competition entry forms?
6 How did the poems and entry forms get posted?
7 Where was the winning poem to be published?
8 Where and when did the ponytrekking start?
9 Why didn't Emma know that Rochelle had been declared the winner?
10 When did Rochelle realise that it wasn't her poem that had won?

Work out answers to these questions.
1 Where were they able to spend time with horses?
2 What kind of prizes were usually given in the Children's Poetry Competition?
3 They were 'scratching their heads' (line 28): Why?
4 Which of the girls read out her poem first?
5 What does 'It' refer to in line 42?
6 How did Rochelle learn that she had won?
7 What does 'it' refer to in line 59?
8 'Rochelle felt really bad' (line 66): What exactly were her feelings, do you think?

B

Supply the missing words. In most cases, the first or last letter(s) of the missing word is (are) given. All the expressions are in the story.
1 I dream o_____ the day when I will have _____ own car.
2 Don't read it to yourself: read it a_____d so that everyone can hear.
3 I saw many homeless people. It m_____ me wonder if anyone cared.
4 Whoever grows the biggest cabbage will w_____ first _____ze.
5 I wish you c_____ _____ been there when I rode the pony.
6 If a thing is w_____ doing, it's w_____ doing well.
7 I'm bored. I tell _____ wh_____: let's take the day o_____ and go horseriding.

77

8 Because you've worked so hard, I have a special t_____ for you: some ice cream!

9 F_____ giving away your wh_____ CD collection! You must be mad!

10 It's such a lovely place. Let's just sit here for a wh_____ and r_____x.

C

Add a word from [I] to a word from [II] to make two-word phrases that will fit in the sentences. We have done the first one to help you. All the expressions are in the story.

[I] bound   can't   go   I   instead   mad   mixed   send   your

[II] about   bet   for   of   round   stand   to   turn   up

1 If you are interested in going to Law School, why don't you *send for* some information?

2 I_____ _____ Wagner's music. It makes me feel like crying.

3 If you work really hard, you're _____ _____ pass your examinations.

4 Aren't you the manager? Sorry, I must have got you _____ _____ with someone else.

5 _____ _____ you can't tell how old I am? Go on, guess!

6 It's _____ _____ to wash the car this week. I did it last week.

7 Sarah is _____ _____ Utrillo. The walls of her room are covered with his paintings.

8 You ought to get more exercise _____ _____ sitting in a chair watching TV all day.

9 Let's _____ _____ to Joe's house and see if he's got any new CDs.

Wordgame

There are several expressions like brand new *meaning* very very new. *Use words from [I] and [II] to complete the sentences. We have done the first one to help you.*

[I] blood   ~~brand~~   dirt   ice   navy   razor   rock

[II] blue   cheap   cold   hard   ~~new~~   red   sharp

1 He must have inherited some money: he's driving a *brand new* Mercedes.

2 The blade of his penknife was _____ _____ ; he almost cut his finger with it.

3 What a hot day! I need a really _____ _____ drink to cool me down.

4 This bread must be about two weeks old: it's completely _____ _____ .

5 Yosef was wearing a _____ _____ suit, the same colour as a sailor's uniform.

6 The sun turned a _____ _____ colour as it sank below the horizon.

7 There must be a sale on here; everything is _____ _____ .

Questions for Discussion

1 What do you think of Rochelle? What would you have done in the same situation?

2 If you were Emma's mother, how would you feel about what had happened?

3 Do you like reading or listening to poetry? What is your favourite kind of poetry?

Say That Again

GLOSSARY

sound your horn (line 4): let the other motorist know you are angry with them.

Unlike poor Arthur Bridge (line 8): Arthur Bridge has not been lucky.

trainees (line 10): people who are learning how to do a particular job.

from all over the world (line 10): from many different countries.

His visit was taken very seriously (line 19): everyone felt that his visit was very important.

as the evening wore on (lines 25–6): as it got later into the evening.

Silence fell on the company (lines 26–7): The company – the people present – stopped talking.

keep the conversation going (line 28): find something else to talk about.

equally keen to break the embarrassing silence (line 33): he wanted to keep the conversation going as much as I did.

at last (lines 39–40): finally, after everything else was finished.

to rejoin his company (line 41): to go back to the company he worked for.

neared completion (line 43): was almost finished.

he vaguely remembered (lines 45–6): he remembered very little.

dragged on (lines 50–1): the time passed slowly because conversation was so difficult.

the usual topics had been exhausted (lines 51–2): there was nothing more to say about them.

Spacing his words out (lines 58–9): Speaking very slowly and clearly.

LANGUAGE PRACTICE

A

Look at the story and find answers to these questions.

1 Why would the woman at the party be upset?
2 What do people learn about at Dr Schumann's institute?
3 Why did Arthur go to Wolfsburg?
4 Who were the six people who also visited Wolfsburg on the day that Arthur went there?
5 Where was the restaurant, and who went to it that evening?
6 What did they talk about during the early part of the evening?
7 What did the man sitting next to Arthur look like?
8 How much did Arthur understand of the man's answer?
9 How did Arthur feel when he got back to his hotel? Why?
10 Who were the people at the dinner on Arthur's second visit?

Work out answers to these questions.

1 What two things had the group of German companies been asked to do?
2 Why do you think they chose Arthur Bridge to go to Wolfsburg? (three reasons).
3 Why do you think Arthur's visit was 'taken very seriously' (line 19)?
4 What made conversation so difficult in the later part of the evening?

5 Why was the man so keen to answer Arthur's question?
6 Do you think Arthur really knew nothing about German wines?
7 Why did the man sitting next to Arthur 'space out his words' when he replied (lines 58–9)?
8 How do we know it was the same man that he had asked before?

B

Supply the missing words. In most cases, the first or last letter(s) of the missing word is (are) given. All the expressions are in the story.

1 I wished the gr_____ would open and _____ow me up.
2 He travelled a_____ over the world in s_____ch of the perfect woman.
3 Birdwatchers t_____ their hobby very s_____y.
4 Schweitzer was not _____y a doctor but a_____ a very good musician.
5 Where _____ld you like to go _____ dinner this evening?
6 Everyone was so tired that it was really difficult to k_____ the conversation _____.
7 He's an intelligent man, but, to tell the tr_____, I f_____ his conversation rather boring.
8 I knew nothing _____ Hannover, but it didn't m_____ because I had a guidebook with me.
9 The sooner you stop smoking, the _____. Find something e_____ to sp_____d your money on.
10 What's the m_____ with you? You l_____k as _____f you h_____ seen a ghost.

C

Use the verb in brackets to complete the sentences. All the verbs are in the story.

Example: Amanda _____ it was a mistake to ask such a question. (know)

Amanda *knew* it was a mistake to ask such a question.

1 He _____ German, but couldn't speak it very well. (understand)
2 This plant was _____ by a group of German companies. (build)
3 Arthur asked him what all the different names _____. (mean)

4 The man was very nervous, and _____ looking at his watch. (keep)

5 Arthur was _____ by his company to report on the training. (send)

6 The man in glasses _____ Arthur all about German wines. (tell)

7 The hotel was quite close so it only _____ five minutes to walk back. (take)

8 Arthur _____ he recognised some of the people at the table. (think)

9 Everyone _____ very embarrassed because of the long silence. (feel)

10 I've _____ my glasses. Where can I get them repaired? (break)

Wordgame
Add items from the two columns to make complete words. All the words are in the story.
Example: *luck-* + *-y* makes *lucky*.

1 chem-   -al
2 excel-   -ation
3 explan-   -ent
4 mom-   -ic
5 real-   -id
6 sever-   -ise
7 stup-   -istry
8 top-   -lent

Questions for Discussion
1 Why did Arthur make such a mistake? What could he have done to avoid it?
2 The story is about embarrassing moments. What was your most embarrassing moment?
3 When you say something embarrassing, how do you put it right? What do you think Arthur did?

April Fool

GLOSSARY

April Fool (title): On April 1st, people try to play tricks on each other, to make them into an April Fool.

Elizabeth's face fell (line 4): she began to look unhappy.

be off to work (line 12): leave for work.

they had their heads together (line 19): they were whispering to each other.

What's the matter with her? (line 26): what's wrong with her?

passed in every subject (line 31): was successful in the examination in every subject.

private lessons (line 43): lessons with a private teacher that have to be paid for.

if you ask me (lines 46–7): in my opinion.

pay their father back (line 49): do to him what he had done to them – play a trick on him.

lawn (line 51): an area of well-kept grass around a house.

From a distance (line 53): they were far away so they could not be seen clearly.

molehills (line 54): the piles of earth that a mole throws up as it digs its tunnel below the ground.

He began to swear (line 58): he began to use bad words.

He turned on them (line 60): he spoke to them angrily.

official-looking (line 64): it did not look like a personal letter from a friend, etc.

LANGUAGE PRACTICE

A

Look at the story and find answers to these questions.

1 Why was Elizabeth's blue file so important to her?
2 How did William react to the trick his father had played on Elizabeth?
3 What did the father say about his son's shirt?
4 Where was mother when the children left the house?

5 What did Elizabeth do when her father gave her the letter from the Examinations Board?
6 Why was Elizabeth so upset at her father's reaction to her news?
7 Why was Elizabeth taking private lessons?
8 What trick did the children play on their father?
9 What made Father swear?
10 How did Mother feel when she heard that Elizabeth had passed her French examination?

Work out answers to these questions.
1 At what time of day does the story begin?
2 What was wrong with William's shirt?
3 What do you think the children were talking about as they walked down the road?
4 What was 'the matter with' Elizabeth (line 26)?
5 Do you think Elizabeth was pleased with what she found in the envelope?
6 'Mother shook her head' (line 39) Why?
7 Why do you think Father was against Elizabeth's having private lessons?
8 Why do you think Elizabeth didn't want her father to know about her French result?

B

Supply the missing words. In most cases, the first or last letter(s) of the missing word is (are) given. All the expressions are in the story.
1 Sheep look quite pretty from a d_____e, but they are ugly when you get close.
2 If you p_____ your examination, you will go up to the next class.
3 But if you f_____ your examination, you will have to repeat the year.
4 What's _____ m_____ _____ William? Is he ill?
5 His face f_____ when he saw wh_____ the moles _____ done to his lawn.
6 I must be o_____ now or I will be late _____ school.
7 It's a w_____ of time talking to him; he never listens.

8 I shall be in tr_____ if I _____ not finish this homework
  b_____ tomorrow morning.
9 I got 8 out of 9 subjects: I passed in e_____y subject,
  ex_____ History.
10 Go u_____s and bring d_____n the book that is on my
  bedside table.

C

Put the words in brackets in their usual place in the sentence.
Example: Have you seen a mole? (ever)
         Have you *ever* seen a mole?
1 People like to play tricks on April the first. (on each other)
2 The two children left the house. (together)
3 The envelope contained something important. (obviously)
4 She came a few minutes later. (down)
5 He turned on them. (angrily)
6 We wanted to play a trick on you. (just)
7 Someone must have thrown it. (away)
8 Everyone was sitting at the table. (silently)
9 Let's pay Father for the trick he played on us. (back)
10 They got up on the morning of the first. (early)

Wordgame
There are many expressions in English like dig up *(line 58). Use these
five verbs with* away, back, off *or* up *to complete the sentences. All the
expressions are in the story.*
clear take pay pick throw
away back off up up
1 Please _____ _____ any bits of paper you see lying on the
  ground and put them in the dustbin.
2 They wanted to _____ their father _____ for the trick he
  had played on them.
3 You must _____ _____ the mess you have made.
4 Don't _____ those empty boxes _____ ; I need them to put
  my books in.
5 They told him to _____ _____ his jacket and put it on the
  chair.

Questions for Discussion

1 Elizabeth and her father don't seem to get on well together. Why do you think this is?
2 When Elizabeth said: 'Mummy, don't tell him' (line 68), how do you think her mother reacted?
3 Do you have a custom like April Fool's Day? What kinds of tricks do people play on each other?

Soap

GLOSSARY

ripened (line 3): from the adjective *ripe* – ready to pick or eat.

wink (line 6): shut one eye quickly to send a message, for example, a secret.

studied herself from every angle (line 12): looked at herself closely, front, back and sides.

chatting (line 13): making polite conversation.

were heaped with good food (line 15): had big amounts of good food on them.

All that was missing (line 16): the only thing that was not there.

might not take any notice of her at all (lines 20–1): might ignore her completely.

the size of peaches (line 26): as big as peaches.

The first pressing (line 28): The first time the olives are squeezed to get the oil from them.

what about the soap? (line 32): now, tell us about the soap.

a thousand times over (line 34): we shall be able to wash each pair of feet a thousand times.

'*Waste not, want not*' (line 35): a proverb: don't waste things and you won't be short of anything.

football pitch (line 39): the field where a football game is played.

tightrope (line 41): a high rope in a circus which acrobats walk along. It looks very dangerous.

skip and hop (line 42): ways of walking; 'to skip' is make little jumps; 'to hop' is to walk on one leg.

What on earth . . . (line 51): used to express great surprise.

What . . . were you thinking of? (line 51): what made you do that?

Today of all days (line 53): today, for you, is the most important
  day of all the days in the year.

LANGUAGE PRACTICE

A

Look at the story and find answers to these questions.

 1 What kind of weather is needed to ripen olives?
 2 What did her father's wink tell Zeynep?
 3 When was Zeynep's birthday party to take place?
 4 What kind of dress did her father buy for her?
 5 What did the guests do while they were waiting?
 6 What was Zeynep worried about as she looked at herself in the
    mirror?
 7 How is the soap made?
 8 What games do the children play round the soap container?
 9 How did Zeynep get out of the soap container?
10 What was it that Zeynep's father couldn't understand?

Work out answers to these questions.

 1 Why was it such an excellent year for olives?
 2 Why do you think Zeynep looked in 'every mirror' (line 11)?
 3 Why do you think Zeynep 'wanted to be alone for a while' (lines
    17–18)?
 4 What made her feel 'like a filmstar' (lines 19–20)?
 5 Why does someone say 'Waste not, want not' to Osman?
 6 Why do you think nobody reacted to the first scream?
 7 In what way was Zeynep 'a mess' (lines 49–50)?
 8 Why do you think Zeynep took the risk of falling into the soap?

B

*Add a word(s) from [I] to a word(s) from [II] to make phrases that will
fit in the sentences. We have done the first one to help you. All the
expressions are in the story.*

[I] half at for in just ~~looked at~~ on take today of what
[II] about a word a while all all days any notice enough
      earth ~~himself~~ the size

87

1 William *looked at himself* in the mirror to make sure his hair was tidy.
2 Where _____ did you buy that silly hat?
3 I'm almost broke, but I have _____ money to buy one more ice cream.
4 Don't _____ of what he says; he rarely tells the truth.
5 She's kind and helpful and patient. _____, a treasure.
6 If you're not feeling well, why don't you go and lie down _____?
7 Our back lawn is quite big: about _____ of a baseball field
8 Don't be late for school, _____, when you have an examination!
9 The dog is fine, but _____ the cat? She hasn't eaten anything _____.

C

Rewrite the sentence starting with the word(s) given in brackets. All the expressions are in the story.
Example: I don't have a car but I know how to drive. (Although . . .)
　　　Although I don't have a car, I know how to drive.

1 They made the soap from the olive skins. (They used the . . .)
2 I have never seen such a pretty dress! (That is the . . .)
3 He smiled and that is how she knew he was pleased with her. (She knew from . . .)
4 He didn't really know why he had written the letter. (He wrote the letter without . . .)
5 The oily liquid had ruined her dress. (Her dress . . .)
6 They shouted to Zeynep: 'Hop along the wall!' (They dared . . .)
7 Everything was there except the bread. (All that . . .)
8 'When does the party begin?' they asked. (They were waiting . . .)
9 I cannot understand why you did such a thing! (Why on earth . . . ?)
10 No one could remember a better harvest. (It was the . . .)

Wordgame
In these sentences, two words have been put in the wrong way round. For example, the sentence 'In the garden front, people were sitting

round chatting', *should be* 'In the <u>front garden</u> . . .' *Correct the other sentences. All the expressions are in the story.*

1 Everyone agreed that it had been an excellent harvest olive.
2 The soap container was about half the size of a pitch football.
3 They pretended they were on a tightrope circus when they walked along the container wall.
4 Poor Zeynep's dress silk was ruined when she fell into the liquid soap.
5 The rain spring and the autumn sun produced a wonderful crop of olives that year.

Questions for Discussion
1 What do you think Zeynep and her father said to each other about the day's events?
2 The people in the story are celebrating Zeynep's birthday. How are birthdays celebrated in your country?
3 'People often do silly things without knowing why' (lines 56–7). Do you agree?

It Will Do You Good

GLOSSARY

'*Eat up, Philip.*' (line 3): the word 'up' is added to give the meaning: 'Eat everything, finish eating'.

be any trouble to you (line 12): cause you any problems.

you'd better take (line 13): you ought to take.

Clutching his stomach (line 17): Holding his stomach tightly to show that he is in pain.

a dose of Sulman's (line 28): some of Sulman's Stomach Medicine.

there was no escape (line 31): there was no way out of the situation.

the front room (line 32): the 'best room', used only for special occasions.

spoonful (line 34): as much as you can hold in a spoon. Note that the plural is *spoonfuls*.

bitterly (line 38): he felt bitter, angry, upset.

crouching down (line 41): bending low with his legs doubled.

pussy (line 46): a child's word for 'cat'.

purred (line 46): 'purring' is the sound made by a cat when it is happy, or thinks it could be happy soon.

miaowed (line 49): 'miaowing' is the sound made by a cat; in this case it miaowed to say 'Yes, please'.

sniff at (line 51): smell something to find out if it is all right.

lap it up (line 51): 'lap' describes the way cats and other animals drink using their tongue.

mighty (line 54): very very strong and loud.

stood on end (line 55): all the hairs on her back stood up, as on a brush.

shot (line 57): moved very very quickly, like a bullet shot from a gun.

LANGUAGE PRACTICE

A

Look at the story and find answers to these questions.

1 What was special about the day at school?
2 What words in the text tell us that Philip was not really in pain?
3 What did Philip like about doing nothing?
4 When did he finally get out of bed?
5 What is 'Sulman's', and what is it like?
6 How much Sulman's was Philip supposed to take?
7 What did he intend to do with his dose of Sulman's?
8 What does the word 'it' refer to in line 49?
9 What does the word 'that' refer to in line 60?
10 What does Philip's mother say about the yoghurt she gives him?

Work out answers to these questions.

1 Where are Philip and his mother when the story opens, do you think?
2 What finally convinces his mother that he is ill?
3 Why did Philip ask if he could take the Sulman's in the front room, do you think?
4 What is Philip's theory about the result of taking Sulman's?
5 How does the cat test the Sulman's?
6 How would you describe the cat's reaction after she drank the Sulman's?

7 How does Philip explain the cat's strange behaviour?
8 Do you think that Philip likes yoghurt?

B

Choose a phrase *from [II] to complete the sentence in [I]. All the expressions are in the story. We have done one to help you: you need phrase vii to complete sentence 3* – The trouble with being ill is that you have to take awful medicine.

[I]		[II]
1 The film was so frightening that	i	all his friends were working.
2 He felt a pain in his leg so	ii	it made the cat spin round and round.
3 ~~The trouble with being ill is that~~	iii	it made his hair stand on end.
4 The medicine tasted so awful that	iv	he stretched it out as far as it would go.
5 He was feeling so much better that	v	he'd better take the day off school.
6 He didn't want to take the test so	vi	he decided to get up and go downstairs.
7 He shouted so loudly that	vii	~~you have to take awful medicine.~~
8 As he was ill, his mother said that	viii	it could be heard at the other end of the street.
9 He enjoyed lying in bed because	ix	he pretended to be ill.

C

There are two mistakes in each of these sentences to be corrected. All the expressions are in the story.

Example: He *come* into the front room and put the bottle *at* the table.

He *came* into the front room and put the bottle *on* the table.

1 Come on, Philip, hurry up, or you're late in school.
2 He groaned again, lied his head on the table as if he was just died.

3 Sorry, mum, I'll be all right. I don't want be no trouble to you.
4 He even could convince himself that he had a bad pain in her stomach.
5 What pity it happen today of all days, when you have an examination.
6 Off you go in bed, and don't got up until you're feeling better.
7 It feels good to lay in bed doing nothing while everyone other is working.
8 My stomach feels very better now that I have take a dose of Sulman's.
9 The cat was very interesting in what Philip was doing the medicine with.
10 She shoot out of the room and was not seeing again till the end of the day.

Wordgame
There are several useful words in English like spoonful *(line 34). Rewrite these sentences using a word ending in -ful. Start with the word(s) given in brackets. We have done the first one as an example.*

1 Take your medicine – as much as a spoon will hold. (Take a . . .)
   Take a spoonful of medicine.
2 He was holding a lot of coins in his hand. (He had . . .)
3 She was carrying a lot of flowers in her arm. (She had . . .)
4 You will need to add water – as much as a cup will hold. (Add . . .)
5 She couldn't answer because she had a lot of sweets in her mouth. (She had . . .)
6 The boys had a lot of apples in their pockets. (They had . . .)

Questions for Discussion
1 Do you think Philip was cruel to the cat?
2 If you were Philip, how would you explain your absence to your schoolfriends next day?
3 'Why is it that everything you like is bad for you?' (line 37). Do you agree? Give examples.

A Perfectly Natural Explanation

GLOSSARY

for no apparent reason (line 1): for no reason that anyone could see.

rocking chair (line 3): a chair which rocks, moves backwards and forwards.

offered explanations (lines 8–9): tried to find something to explain what had happened.

not a breath of wind (line 11): no wind at all.

a tough old bird (line 21): a very healthy woman despite her age.

fitter (line 21): 'fit' is in good physical condition; 'healthy' means free from illness.

get my own back (lines 24–5): do to her what she had done to me.

idle threats (line 29): threats which they would not carry out.

frightened out of our wits (line 50): very very frightened; 'wits' is an old word similar in meaning to 'mind'.

get over it (line 51): recover from the shock.

I was in on the joke (lines 57–8): I knew his secret.

as white as a sheet (line 61): *very* pale.

LANGUAGE PRACTICE

A

Look at the story and find answers to these questions.

1 What kind of picture was hanging on the wall?
2 Why was the writer proud of himself?
3 How did the writer get his own back on his sister?
4 What was Mother's 'idle threat' to the children?
5 Why did Grandma Pye look as if she was about to slip off her chair?
6 How do we know Betty was frightened when the picture moved again?
7 What did Mother do after the picture moved again?
8 'Betty and I crept downstairs' (line 47). Why did they creep?
9 How did the writer find out that his father had played a trick on them?
10 How did the family get the news about Grandma Pye's death?

Work out answers to these questions.

1 What made people notice that the picture had moved?
2 Why couldn't Father's explanation be correct?
3 Why was the writer so sure that his grandmother was all right?
4 'Perhaps it's a sign?' (line 23). What did Betty mean by that?
5 What does the word 'that' in line 29 refer to?
6 What do you think the writer learned from the bits of conversation he overheard?
7 Why did the writer get up early the following morning, do you think?
8 What was the meaning of the winks that passed between father and son?

B

Fill the gaps in these sentences with A, B or C. All the patterns are in the story.

1 We couldn't understand what had made the picture _____.
   A move   B moving   C to move
2 We _____ if anything had happened to grandma.
   A knew   B were knowing   C would have known
3 She looked as if she was just about _____ over.
   A fall   B to fall   C falling
4 I felt as if we _____ for the first time.
   A have met   B met   C were meeting
5 I _____ sent to get some bread while my sister laid the table.
   A am   B was   C have been
6 I heard my parents still _____ about the mystery.
   A to talk   B talk   C talking
7 As we sat _____ our coffee, Father told us about the phone-call.
   A drinking   B drink   C drinks
8 We stood outside the door trying _____ what they were saying.
   A hear   B to hear   C hearing
9 Come on, _____ ready for school, or you'll be late.
   A get   B to get   C getting

10 When I saw the string, I realised that Dad _____ a trick on
   us.

   A played   B has played   C had played

C

*Replace the words underlined with an expression from the text based on
the word(s) given in brackets. Make any necessary grammatical changes.*

Example: Don't <u>worry</u>! (fuss)

              Don't make a fuss!

1 It was perfectly still outside, <u>no wind at all</u>. (breath)
2 And then he jumped out of the window, <u>and we didn't know
   why</u>. (apparent)
3 I was able to swim when I was <u>much much younger than you
   are now</u>. (half)
4 The sudden noise nearly frightened me <u>very much</u>. (wits)
5 I was very upset at first but I soon <u>forgot all about it</u>. (over)
6 I winked at my father to let him know that I <u>knew about his
   trick</u>. (in on)
7 When he looked again, he noticed that the rabbit <u>wasn't there
   any more</u>. (longer)
8 If you do something bad to me, I will <u>do something bad to you
   in return</u>. (own back)

Wordgame

*There are a lot of expressions in English like 'as white as a sheet' (line
61). Complete these expressions by matching word(s) from [I] and [II].
We have done the first one to help you.*

1 ~~as white as~~   i   ice
2 as cold as   ii   a horse
3 as green as   iii a picture
4 as pretty as   iv   toast
5 as hungry as   v   ~~a sheet~~
6 as warm as   vi   grass

Questions for Discussion

1 Do you think the trick that Father played on the children
   was funny? How do you think their mother felt about the
   trick?

2 'It is another of those habits that make parents such a mystery to their children' (lines 46–7). Can you think of any other examples?

3 Do you like mysteries? Has anything ever happened to you which you couldn't explain?

The Purple Bamboo Park

GLOSSARY

in a way (line 3): this is partly the reason, but not the whole reason.

a proper routine (lines 5–6): regular habits.

early on (line 6): when she first started writing.

fewer people about (line 10): not so many people there.

catch glimpses (line 16): see them from time to time, but only briefly.

got on like a house on fire (line 24): got on very very well.

. . . somehow (line 32): in a way that I cannot explain.

clear off! (line 46): an impolite way to tell someone to go away.

without warning (line 50): she was not expecting it.

laid out (line 50): knocked him to the ground.

karate chop (line 51): using the hand with a chopping movement like an axe to deliver a blow.

LANGUAGE PRACTICE

A

Look at the story and find answers to these questions.

1 Where does Yunhua live?
2 Why does she prefer to go to the park in the evening?
3 Can you describe a bamboo plant?
4 Where did Yunhua meet Charles?
5 Who were 'like ghosts' (line 17)?
6 How did Charles react to the park? Why?
7 How were the three young men dressed?
8 How did Charles react to the young men? Why?
9 How did Yunhua get rid of the three men?
10 What did Charles and Yunhua do after the young men had fled?

Work out answers to these questions.
1 What is Yunhua's 'proper routine'?
2 How does the park get its name?
3 Why is everything in the park 'half-seen' (line 15)?
4 What does the text tell you about *tai chi*?
5 Why was Yunhua invited to the reception?
6 Did the tall young man really want a light for his cigarette?
7 Why did Charles look at Yunhua 'open-mouthed' (line 53)?
8 'I didn't bother to answer his question' (line 55). Why not?

B

Add words from [I] and [II] to make phrases that will fit in the sentences.
We have done the first one to help you. All the expressions are in the
story.

[I] a house   caught   clear   didn't   early   fell   face   laid
~~regular~~   without
[II] a glimpse   bother   ~~breaks~~   in love   off   on   on fire   out
to face   warning

1 Don't sit at your computer for hours; you must take *regular*
breaks.
2 They met when they were in Paris, _____ and were married
a month later.
3 I was standing on the platform when, _____, a man came
up and hit me.
4 Children learn _____ that they have to say please and thank
you.
5 The man asked me for money but I just told him to _____.
6 It was so dark that I only _____ of the car as it sped past
me.
7 She _____ the tall man with a single blow.
8 It was such a stupid letter that I _____ to reply to it.
9 My boss is a wonderful person; she and I get on like _____.
10 We have spoken on the phone many times, but we have never
met _____.

C

Rewrite the sentence starting with the word(s) given in brackets. All the
expressions are in the story.

Example: I don't have a car but I know how to drive. (Although . . .)
   Although I don't have a car, I know how to drive.

1 Very few Chinese writers are well known outside China. (She was one . . .)
2 Penguin has published some of my books. (Some . . .)
3 Regular habits are important for a writer. (It is important . . .)
4 The Ambassador's wife invited me to an embassy reception. (I . . .)
5 We went to the park; we didn't meet again after that. (The last time . . .)
6 I go there in the evening when there are fewer people about. (The reason I . . .)
7 Having only recently arrived, he didn't know anyone. (He didn't . . .)
8 The house is called Sequoia because of the big trees round it. (The name . . .)

Wordgame
In each sentence, there are two words which have a letter missing. For example, the sentence 'The Bamboo ark is a strange pace' *should be* 'The Bamboo <u>park</u> is a strange <u>place</u>.' *Find and correct the words that have a letter missing. All the words are used in the story.*

1 When you wok with computers, it is important to take regular beaks.
2 I wet to night school to lean karate.
3 The two offices got on like a hose on fire.
4 When the young man tied to grab me, I gave him a kick to the had.
5 He sad goodnight and let me standing in the street.

Questions for Discussion
1 What do you think about the way Charles behaved? What would you have done in his position?
2 Would you have reacted as Yunhua reacted to Charles's fear?
3 How do you think Charles felt after the event? Do you feel sorry for him? What advice would you give him?

First Impressions

GLOSSARY

make an appointment (line 4): arrange a time to see me.

very urgent (line 5): it is something which cannot wait.

thickset (line 7): heavy, but not fat.

Put it this way (line 12): Let me make it clearer by saying it another way or by adding something.

first impressions (line 12): what you notice about someone the first time you meet them.

regional accent (line 30): people in different parts (regions) of the country speak the national language with a different accent.

So what? (line 30): What difference does that make?

speck (line 42): a very small bit of dirt.

your people (lines 58–9): the police.

'The game's up' (lines 59–60): You have found out about me.

shoes or no shoes (line 65): whether I am careful about my shoes or not.

LANGUAGE PRACTICE

A

Look at the story and find answers to these questions.

1 What did the visitor look like?
2 Why did Hedley decide to answer the visitor's question?
3 What three things does Hedley first notice about a person?
4 What does the word 'it' refer to in line 20?
5 What did Hedley mean by 'correctly' (line 31)?
6 What were Hedley's shoes like?
7 What did Hedley first notice about the visitor's shoes?
8 Was Hedley surprised by the discovery that the visitor was a police officer?
9 What crime does the police officer want to talk about?
10 Hedley 'had not been careful enough' (lines 64–5). Careful about what?

Work out answers to these questions.

1 Who is talking to Hedley when the story opens, do you think?
2 Why, according to the visitor, don't clothes tell you much about a person?
3 What did Hedley notice about the visitor's suit?
4 What is Hedley's opinion about regional accents?
5 Do many people make those mistakes? How do you know?
6 What connection is there between Hedley's shoes and his character, do you think?
7 When did Hedley realise that the visitor was a police officer?
8 Why hadn't Hedley realised right away that the visitor was a police officer?

B

There are two mistakes in each of these sentences to be corrected. All the expressions are in the story.

1 He doesn't want tell you now. He says he will explain everything when he will see you.
2 He knew that the police was going to visit him soon or later.
3 Hedley thought he would better answering the stranger's questions.
4 I belief you're a very hardworking man and a very careful, too.
5 You cannot judge of people by the way how they dress.
6 I cannot stand people who they speak with strong regional accent.
7 Hedley looked for his visitor's suit: it was smart but ordinarily.
8 Hedley is the sort of man who like to keep all his things by good condition.
9 Why fashions change so quick nowadays?
10 Does he really thinks he can tell anything about me by looking my shoes?

C

Use the verb in brackets to complete the sentences. All the verbs are in the story.

Example: Joe said he hadn't _____ his brother for ages. (see)
        Joe said he hadn't *seen* his brother for ages.

1 We had a quarrel last year, and we haven't _____ to each other since. (speak)

2 How many times have I _____ you not to wear your hat in bed? (tell)

3 I _____ you were in Paris. When did you get back? (think)

5 Everyone _____ up when the teacher came into the room. (stand)

6 Have you _____ my brother? (meet)

7 Do you like my coat? It's the first time I've _____ it. (wear)

8 The door opened and a tall dark man _____ into the room. (come)

9 I suddenly _____ ill so I went to lie down on my bed. (feel)

10 Have you _____ your application form off yet? (send)

Wordgame
Use these words to fill the gaps in the sentences. All the expressions are used in the story.

correctly   exactly   quickly   really   regularly

1 What _____ do you want?

2 I've never _____ thought about it.

3 Fashions change very _____ nowadays.

4 I don't like to people who don't speak _____ .

5 I clean my teeth _____ , at least twice a day.

Questions for Discussion

1 What do you notice when you first meet someone? What do you think about the shoe theory?

2 Are there things about people that you 'can't stand' (line 34)?

3 Do you think you can tell anything about a person from their star sign?

Seeing is Believing

GLOSSARY

'*Seeing is believing*' (title): a saying: if you see something, it must be real, true.

one day (line 1): at some time in the future.

chimpanzees (line 1): small African apes.

'pigs will fly' (line 3): a saying, used to show you don't think something will happen.

grunted (line 4): made a noise to show he disagreed.

if you like (line 4): if you want to.

not necessarily (line 11): it may be true or it may not.

Coney Island (line 13): a seaside resort in New York with unusual sideshows, begun in the 1840s.

a difficult mission (lines 15–16): for him, it was as difficult as soldiers going on a military mission.

on his own (line 16): alone, by himself.

a fake (line 26): something which is not what it seems to be.

bowed to the wishes (line 29): they agreed to do what she wanted.

hind legs (lines 31–2): back legs.

after a fashion (line 35): in a way that was not perfect, but was not bad either.

drove a hard bargain (lines 40–1): 'to bargain' is to argue over the price of something.

After all . . . (line 41) an expression meaning: 'You have to realise/remember . . .'

his livelihood (line 41): the work from which he earned the money to live.

refused to take no for an answer (line 42): An expression meaning 'insisted'.

propose (line 54): intend.

was not willing to (line 55): would not agree to.

put the dog to sleep (lines 58–9): an expression used to avoid saying that he killed the dog.

doggie (line 65): a child's way of saying 'dog'; the ending -ie or -y means 'dear little'.

LANGUAGE PRACTICE

A

Look at the story and find answers to these questions.

1 What is Professor Smith's theory about apes?

2 What did Professor Jones think about Smith's theory?

3 Why might you think that the two men do not like each other?
4 Why did Smith go to Coney Island?
5 Why did Jones go with him?
6 In what way could the dog 'count'?
7 In what way could the dog 'speak'?
8 Why did Smith put the dog to sleep?
9 What did he find when he examined the dog's brain?
10 Why did Smith's niece come into the room?

Work out answers to these questions.
1 What is the difference between 'facts' and 'ideas' for these two men?
2 For Smith, it was 'a difficult mission' (lines 15–16). Why, do you think?
3 What is Smith's opinion of Coney Island? How do you know?
4 What impressed Smith most about the dog?
5 Did Smith pay a lot for the dog, do you think?
6 What does the niece think when her uncle buys the dog?
7 What does Jones think about what Smith has done to the dog? How do you know?
8 How did the two men react when the little girl asked to play with the dog?

B

Replace the words underlined with an expression from the text based on the word(s) given in brackets. Make any necessary grammatical changes.
Example: Don't <u>worry</u>! (fuss)
        Don't make a fuss!

1 The showman <u>tried to get as much money as possible</u>. (drive/bargain)
2 He <u>didn't trust</u> anything which he could not see. (suspicious)
3 They will <u>be able to do everything that</u> human beings <u>can do</u>. (catch up)
4 'I'm going to give up smoking.' I replied: '<u>I don't believe it will happen</u>.' (day/pigs)
5 He <u>refused</u> to tell us what he was going to do. (willing)
6 The man didn't want to go out, but his friend <u>insisted</u>. (take/answer)

7 Please come with me, I don't want to go <u>alone</u>. (own)
8 They <u>never seemed to agree</u>. (argue/everything)

C

Choose a phrase from [II] to complete the sentence in [I]. All the expressions are in the story. We have done one to help you: phrase iii completes sentence 6: It is silly to think that apes could ever be like men.

[I]		[II]
1 He hoped to discover the secret	i	so he asked a lot of money for it.
2 He only believed in things	ii	he didn't want to go on his own.
3 You would never guess	iii	~~that apes could ever be like men.~~
4 It looks as if	iv	which might explain the dog's abilities.
5 He wanted to learn more about the dog	v	by the dog's ability to count and speak.
6 ~~It is silly to think~~	vi	which he could see.
7 He was amazed	vii	that they were friends.
8 The showman earned money with the dog	viii	the dog has been very well trained.
9 He couldn't find anything	ix	so he decided to buy it.
10 Smith took his friend Jones, because	x	by examining the dog's brain.

Wordgame
Complete this table. All the words are used in the story.

	Noun	Adjective
Example:	*happiness*	happy
1	_____	able
2	_____	difficult
3	intelligence	_____
4	logic	_____
5	science	_____
6	suspicion	_____

Questions for Discussion

1 Do you think that Professor Smith was right to try to find out why the dog was so clever?
2 Do you only believe in things you can see, hear, smell, taste or touch?
3 Do you think it is right to use animals in circuses? How do you feel when you see animals doing tricks?

A Better Mousetrap

GLOSSARY

mousetrap (title): something used to catch mice.

in centuries (line 1): for hundreds of years.

one such inventor (line 3): one of the inventors who wanted to design a better mousetrap.

Actually (line 7): similar to 'In fact'.

Patent Office (line 13): The place you register inventions, to prevent other people from stealing your idea.

I present (line 16): this expression is normally used to introduce acts in a theatre, etc.

Do go on (line 26): Please continue.

balustrade (line 32): the part of a balcony which prevents people from falling off it.

this is the clever bit (line 38): this is what makes it special and different.

hey presto! (line 40): an expression used by magicians as they perform a trick.

Throat is cut. Mouse is dead (line 40): The blade cuts the mouse's throat, and the mouse dies.

people might find it (lines 45–6): people might feel that it is.

hacksaw (line 57): a saw with very fine and very sharp teeth, used for cutting metal.

stroke of genius (line 61): a very clever idea, something no one else would have thought of.

LANGUAGE PRACTICE

A

Look at the story and find answers to these questions.

1 What made Mandini think about the present design of the mousetrap?
2 What had Mandini been using a mousetrap for?
3 Mandini 'found himself in a waiting room'. What was he waiting for?
4 Where was he holding the cardboard box?
5 How does the mouse get to the balcony?
6 How is the mouse supposed to be killed in the Mandini Mark I mousetrap?
7 What three things, according to the Patent Officer, were wrong with the Mark I mousetrap?
8 How long did it take Mandini to produce a new design?
9 What was Mandini's 'stroke of genius' (line 61)?
10 Where was the hacksaw blade fitted?

Work out answers to these questions.

1 Was Mandini a successful inventor? How do you know?
2 How long did it take Mandini to design his own mousetrap? Was it an easy job?
3 What was the Patent Officer's immediate reaction to Mandini's mousetrap?
4 Why do you think the Patent Officer felt he was 'getting too old for this job' (line 42)?
5 What was the Patent Officer's immediate reaction to the Mark II mousetrap?
6 What features did the Mark II have that were also in the first version?
7 What did the Patent Officer think of Mandini's 'stroke of genius'?
8 What was, in theory, the effect of not putting any cheese in the trap?

B

Supply the missing words in this passage. In most cases the first or last letter(s) of the missing word is (are) given.

I knew a man once who i_____d a trap for c_____ elephants. He took his design to the Patent Office in a ca_____d box, and pr_____y presented it to the Patent Officer. 'Please ex_____ _____ me how it w_____s,' said the Patent Officer. The man opened the box and t_____ out a sheet of paper, an empty bottle and a telescope. 'I don't qu_____ understand.' 'It's very si_____e,' said the man. 'You look through the wrong end of the telescope to m_____ the elephant small, then you put the elephant i_____ the bottle.' 'But how do you know that the elephant will st_____d still long enough for you to c_____ it?' 'This is the cl_____ bit. You write 2 + 2 = 5 on the p_____ of paper, and the elephant will stop, because it is puzzled. That's when you gr_____b it!'

C

Rewrite the sentence starting with the word(s) given in brackets. All the expressions are in the story.

Example: I don't have a car but I know how to drive. (Although . . .)
   Although I don't have a car, I know how to drive.

1 It only works if there is cheese in it. (It depends . . .)
2 The job was too much for him at his age. (He was . . .)
3 I don't think it will catch mice. (I doubt . . .)
4 He became rich from his inventions. (His inventions . . .)
5 What's the difference between mice and rats? (In what way . . . ?)
6 He didn't use cheese, he used a piece of apple. (Instead of . . .)
7 He said how amazed he was. (He expressed . . .)
8 The hole has the word DOOR written over it. (The word . . .)
9 It sees a piece of cheese on the floor below. (What . . .)
10 He had fitted a razorblade on the top. (The razorblade which he . . .)

Wordgame
Complete the tables. All the words are in the story.

	Verb	Noun
1	invent	_____
2	_____	injury
3	_____	explanation
4	differ	_____
5	amaze	_____

	Adjective	Noun
1	_____	use
2	_____	fame
3	_____	triumph
4	_____	pride
5	_____	silence

Questions for Discussion
1 What do you think of Mandini's earlier inventions? Is he mad, or is he a genius?
2 Give your ideas for a better mousetrap.
3 Name five inventions which you think have been very important, and say why you chose them.